When Ben lifted his head from the wave and saw Sandy standing on the beach, it was as if the past and the present had coalesced into one shining moment. A joy so unexpected it was painful had flooded his heart.

So here he was, against all resolutions, kissing her.

Her lips warm and pliant beneath his, her body pressed to his chest. Her eyes, startled at first, and then filled with an expression of bliss.

He shouldn't be kissing her. Starting things he could not finish. Risking pain for both of them. But those thoughts were lost in the wonder of having her close to him again.

It was like the twelve years between kisses had never happened.

Dear Reader,

I'm delighted to be sharing my first book for the Harlequin Romance line with you. I've read and enjoyed so many wonderful romances from Harlequin, it's a particular joy to have the opportunity to write one of my own!

Reunion stories are among my favorites. I so enjoyed reuniting Sandy and Ben years after they first met as teenagers, and exploring the emotional ups and downs of their love story.

I've set their romance on the south coast of New South Wales, Australia. A few hours' drive away from Sydney takes you to pristine beaches, beautiful bushland and quaint towns. The town of Dolphin Bay is my own, but it is inspired by places where I have spent many idyllic holidays. I hope you enjoy spending time there on the pages of *The Summer They Never Forgot*.

Kandy

The Summer They Never Forgot

—

Kandy Shepherd

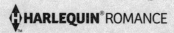

Recycling programs
for this product may
not exist in your area.

ISBN-13: 978-0-373-74279-0

THE SUMMER THEY NEVER FORGOT

First North American Publication 2014

Copyright © 2014 by Kandy Shepherd

Printed in U.S.A.

Kandy Shepherd swapped a fast-paced career as a magazine editor for a life writing romance. She lives on a small farm in the Blue Mountains near Sydney, Australia, with her husband, daughter and a menagerie of animal friends. Kandy believes in love at first sight and real-life romance—they worked for her!

Kandy loves to hear from her readers. Visit her website, at www.kandyshepherd.com.

This is Kandy Shepherd's first book for the Harlequin Romance line, and is available in ebook format from www.Harlequin.com.

CHAPTER ONE

On Sandy Adams's thirtieth birthday—which was also the day the man she'd lived with for two years was getting married to another woman—she decided to run away.

No. Not run away. *Find a new perspective.*

Yes, that sounded good. Positive. Affirming. Challenging.

No way would she give even a second's thought to any more heartbreak.

She'd taken the first step by driving the heck out of Sydney and heading south—her ultimate destination: Melbourne, a thousand kilometres away. On a whim, she'd chosen to take the slower, scenic route to Melbourne on the old Princes Highway. There was time, and it went through areas she thought were among the most beautiful in the state of New South Wales.

Alone and loving it, she repeated to herself as she drove.

Say it enough times and she might even start to believe it.

Somewhere between the seaside town of Kiama and the quaint village of Berry, with home two hours behind her, she pulled her lime-green Beetle off onto a safe lay-by. But she only allowed herself a moment to stretch out her cramped muscles and admire the rolling green hills and breathtaking blue expanse of the Pacific Ocean before she got back in the car. The February heat made it too hot to stay outside for too long.

From her handbag she pulled out her new notebook, a birthday present from her five-year-old niece. There was a pink fairy on the cover and the glitter from its wings had already shed all through Sandy's bag. It came with a shocking-pink pen. She nibbled on the pen for a long moment.

Then, with a flourish, she headed up the page 'Thirtieth Birthday Resolutions' and started to scribble in pink ink.

1. Get as far away from Sydney as possible while remaining in realms of civilisation and within reach of a good latte.

2. Find new job where can be own boss.

She underscored the words 'own boss' three times, so hard she nearly tore the paper.

3. Find kind, interesting man with no hang-ups

*who loves me the way I am and who wants to
get married and have lots of kids.*

She crossed out 'lots of kids' and wrote instead
'three kids'—then added, *'two girls and a boy'*.
When it came to writing down goals there was no
harm in being specific. So she also added, *'Man who
in no way resembles That-Jerk-Jason'*.

She went over the word 'jerk' twice and finished
with the date and an extravagant flourish. Done.

She liked making lists. She felt they gave her
some degree of control over a life that had gone
unexpectedly pear-shaped. But three goals were
probably all she could cope with right now. The
resolutions could be revisited once she'd got to her
destination.

She put the notebook back into her bag and slid
the car back onto the highway.

An hour or so later farmland had made way for
bushland and the sides of the road were lined with
eucalypt forest. Her shoulders ached from driving
and thoughts of a break for something to eat were at
the front of her mind. When she saw the signpost to
Dolphin Bay it took only a second for her to decide
to throw the car into a left turn.

It was a purely reflex action. She'd planned to
stop at one of the beachside towns along the way
for lunch and a swim. But she hadn't given sleepy
Dolphin Bay a thought for years. She'd adored the
south coast when she was a kid—had spent two idyl-

lic summer holidays at different resort towns with her family, revelling in the freedom of being let off the leash of the rigorous study schedule her father had set her during the school year. But one summer the family had stayed in Dolphin Bay for the first time and everything had changed.

At the age of eighteen, she'd fallen in love with Ben. Tall, blond, surfer dude Ben, with the lazy smile and the muscles to die for. He'd been exciting, forbidden and fun. At the same time he'd been a real friend: supportive, encouraging—all the things she'd never dreamed a boy could be.

Then there'd been the kisses. The passionate, exciting, first-love kisses that had surprised her for years afterwards by sneaking into her dreams.

Sandy took her foot off the accelerator pedal and prepared to brake and turn back. She'd closed the door on so many of the bittersweet memories of that summer. Was it wise to nudge it open again by even a fraction?

But how could it hurt to drop in to Dolphin Bay for lunch? It was her birthday, after all, and she couldn't remember the last proper meal she'd eaten. She might even book into Morgan's Guesthouse and stay the night.

She put her foot back to the accelerator, too excited at the thought of seeing Dolphin Bay again to delay any further.

As she cruised into the main street that ran between the rows of shops and the waterfront, excitement melted down in a cold rush of disappointment. She'd made a big mistake. The classic mistake of expecting things to stay the same. She hadn't been to Dolphin Bay for twelve years. And now she scarcely recognised it.

Determined not to give in to any kind of let-down feelings, she parked not far from the wasn't-there-last-time information kiosk, got out, locked the car and walked around, trying to orientate herself.

The southern end of the bay was enclosed by old-fashioned rock sea walls to form a small, safe harbour. It seemed much the same, with a mix of pleasure boats and fishing vessels bobbing on the water. The typically Australian old pub, with its iron lace balconies was the same too.

But gone was the beaten-up old jetty. It had been replaced by a sleek new pier and a marina, a fishing charter business, and a whale- and dolphin-watching centre topped with a large fibreglass dolphin with an inane painted grin that, in spite of her shock, made her smile. Adjoining was a row of upmarket shops and galleries. The fish and chip shop, where she'd squabbled with her sister over the last chip eaten straight from the vinegar-soaked paper, had been pulled down to make way for a trendy café. The dusty general store was now a fashionable boutique.

And, even though it was February and the school holidays were over, there were people strolling, browsing, licking on ice cream cones—more people than she could remember ever seeing in Dolphin Bay.

For a moment disappointment almost won. But she laughed out loud when she noticed the rubbish bins that sat out on the footpath. Each was in the shape of a dolphin with its mouth wide open.

They were absolute kitsch, but she fell in love with them all over again. Surreptitiously, she patted one on its fibreglass snout. 'Delighted you're still here,' she whispered.

Then, when she looked more closely around her, she noticed that in spite of the new sophistication every business still sported a dolphin motif in some form or another, from a discreet sticker to a carved wooden awning.

And she'd bet Morgan's Guesthouse at the northern end of the bay wouldn't have changed. The rambling weatherboard building, dating from the 1920s, would certainly have some sort of a heritage preservation order on it. It was part of the history of the town.

In her mind's eye she could see the guesthouse the way it had been that magic summer. The shuttered windows, the banks of blue and purple hydrangeas her mother had loved, the old sand tennis court where she'd played hit-and-giggle games with Ben. She hoped it hadn't changed too much.

As she approached the tourist information kiosk to ask for directions on how to get there she hesitated. Why did she need the guesthouse to be the same?

Did it have something to do with those rapidly returning memories of Ben Morgan? Ben, nineteen to her eighteen, the surfer hunk all the girls had had wild crushes on.

Around from the bay, accessed via a boardwalk, was a magnificent surf beach. When Ben had ridden his board, harnessing the power of the waves like some suntanned young god, there had always been a giggling gaggle of admiring girls on the sand.

She'd never been one of them. No, she'd stood on the sidelines, never daring to dream he'd see her as anything but a guest staying for two weeks with her family at his parents' guesthouse.

But, to her amazement and joy, he'd chosen *her*. And then the sun had really started to shine that long-ago summer.

'Morgan's Guesthouse?' said the woman manning the information kiosk. 'Sorry, love, I've never heard of it.'

'The old wooden building at the northern end of the bay,' Sandy prompted.

'There's only the Hotel Harbourside there,' the woman said. 'It's a modern place—been there as long as I've been in town.'

Sandy thanked her and walked away, a little confused.

But she gasped when she saw the stark, modern structure of the luxury hotel that had replaced the charming old weatherboard guesthouse. Its roofline paid some kind of homage to the old-fashioned peaked roof that had stood there the last time she had visited Dolphin Bay, but the concrete and steel of its construction did not. The hotel took up the footprint of the original building and gardens, and rose several floors higher.

Hotel Harbourside? She'd call it Hotel Hideous.

She took a deep, calming breath. Then forced herself to think positive. The new hotel might lack the appeal of the old guesthouse but she'd bet it would be air conditioned and would almost certainly have a decent restaurant. Just the place for a solo thirtieth birthday lunch.

And as she stood on the steps that led from the beach to the hotel and closed her eyes, breathed in the salty air, felt the heat shimmering from the sand, listened to the sound of the water lapping at the edge of the breakwater, she could almost imagine everything was the same as it had been.

Almost.

The interior of the restaurant was all glass, steel and smart design. What a difference from the old guesthouse dining room, with its mismatched wooden chairs, well-worn old table and stacks of board games for ruthlessly played after-dinner tournaments. But the windows that looked out over the bay framed a view that was much the same as it had always been—although now a fleet of dolphin-watching boats plied its tourist trade across the horizon.

She found a table in the corner furthest from the bar and sat down. She took off her hat and squashed it in her bag but kept her sunglasses on. Behind them she felt safer. Protected. Less vulnerable, she had to admit to herself.

She refused to allow even a smidgeon of self-pity to intrude as she celebrated her thirtieth birthday all by herself whilst at the same time her ex Jason was preparing to walk down the aisle.

Casting her eye over the menu, Sandy was startled by a burst of masculine laughter over the chatter from the bar. As that sound soared back into her memory her heart gave an excited leap of recognition. No other man's laughter could sound like that.

Rich. Warm. Unforgettable.

Ben.

He hadn't been at the bar when she'd walked in. She'd swear to it. Unless he'd changed beyond all recognition.

She was afraid to look up. Afraid of being disappointed. Afraid of what she might say, do, to the first man to have broken her heart.

Would she go up and say hello? Or put her hat back on and try to slink out without him seeing her?

Despite her fears, she took off her sunglasses with fingers that weren't quite steady and slowly raised her head.

Her breath caught in her throat and she felt the

blood drain from her face. He stood with his profile towards her, but it was definitely Ben Morgan: broad-shouldered, towering above the other men in the bar, talking animatedly with a group of people.

From what she could see from this distance he was as handsome as the day they'd said goodbye. His hair was shorter. He wore tailored shorts and a polo-style shirt instead of the Hawaiian print board shorts and singlet he'd favoured when he was nineteen. He was more muscular. Definitely more grown up.

But he was still Ben.

He said something to the guy standing near him, laughed again at his response. Now, as then, he held the attention of everyone around him.

Did he feel her gaze fixed on him?

Something must have made him turn. As their eyes connected, he froze mid-laugh. Nothing about his expression indicated that he recognised her.

For a long, long moment it seemed as if everyone and everything else in the room fell away. The sound of plates clattering, glasses clinking, and the hum of chatter seemed muted. She realised she was holding her breath.

Ben turned back to the man he'd been talking to, said something, then turned to face her again. This time he smiled, acknowledging her, and she let out her breath in a slow sigh.

He made his way to her table with assured, athletic strides. She watched, mesmerised, taking in the changes wrought by twelve years. The broad-shouldered, tightly muscled body, with not a trace of his teenage gangliness. The solid strength of him. The transformation from boy to man. Oh, yes, the teenage Ben was now very definitely a man.

And hotter than ever.

All her senses screamed that recognition.

He'd reached her before she had a chance to get up from her chair.

'Sandy?'

The voice she hadn't heard for so long was as deep and husky as she remembered. He'd had a man's voice even at nineteen. Though only a year older than her, he'd seemed light years ahead in maturity.

Words of greeting she knew she should utter were wedged in her throat. She coughed. Panicked that she couldn't even manage a hello.

His words filled the void. 'Or are you Alexandra these days?'

He remembered that. Her father had insisted she be called by her full name of Alexandra. But Alexandra was too much of a mouthful, Ben had decided. He'd called her by the name she preferred. From that summer on she'd been Sandy. Except, of course, to her father and mother.

'Who's Alexandra?' she said now, pretending to look around for someone else.

He laughed with what seemed like genuine pleasure to see her. Suddenly she felt her nervousness, her self-consciousness, drop down a notch or two.

She scrambled up from her chair. The small round

table was a barrier between her and the man who'd been everything to her twelve years ago. The man she'd thought she'd never see again.

'It's good to see you, Ben,' she said, her voice still more choked than she would have liked it to be.

His face was the same—strong-jawed and handsome—and his eyes were still as blue as the summer sky at noon. Close-cropped dark blond hair replaced the sun-bleached surfer tangle that so long ago she'd thought was the ultimate in cool. There were creases around his eyes that hadn't been there when he was nineteen. And there was a tiny white crescent of a scar on his top lip she didn't remember. But she could still see the boy in the man.

'It's good to see you, too,' he said, in that so-deep-it-bordered-on-gruff voice. 'I recognised you straight away.'

'Me too. I mean, I recognised you too.'

What did he see as he looked at her? What outward signs had the last years of living life full steam ahead left on her?

'You've cut your hair,' he said.

'So have you,' she said, and he smiled.

Automatically her hand went up to touch her head. Of course he would notice. Her brown hair had swung below her waist when she'd last seen him, and she remembered how he'd made her swear never, *ever* to change it. Now it was cut in a chic, city-smart bob and tastefully highlighted.

'But otherwise you haven't changed,' he added in that husky voice. 'Just grown up.'

'It's kind of you to say that,' she said. But she knew how much she'd changed from that girl that summer.

'Mind if I join you?' he asked.

'Of course. Please. I was just having a drink…'

She sat back down and Ben sat in the chair opposite her. His strong, tanned legs were so close they nudged hers as he settled into place. She didn't draw her legs back. The slight pressure of his skin on her skin, although momentary, sent waves of awareness coursing through her. She swallowed hard.

She'd used to think Ben Morgan was the best-looking man she'd ever seen. The twelve intervening years had done nothing to change her opinion. No sophisticated city guy had ever matched up to him. Not even Jason.

She'd left the menu open on the table before her. 'I see you've decided on dessert before your main meal,' Ben said, with that lazy smile which hadn't changed at all.

'I was checking out the salads, actually,' she lied.

'Really?' he said, the smile still in his voice, and the one word said everything.

He'd caught her out. Was teasing her. Like he'd used to do. With no brothers, an all-girls school and zero dating experience, she hadn't been used to boys. Never hurtful or mean, his happy-go-lucky ways had helped get her over that oversensitivity. It was just one of the ways he'd helped her grow up.

'You're right,' she said, relaxing into a smile. 'Old habits die hard. The raspberry brownie with chocolate fudge sauce *does* appeal.' The birthday cake you had when you weren't having a birthday cake. But she wouldn't admit to that.

'That brownie is so good you'll want to order two servings,' he said.

Like you used to.

The unspoken words hung between them. Their eyes met for a moment too long to be comfortable. She was the first to look away.

Ben signalled the waiter. As he waved, Sandy had to suppress a gasp at the ugly raised scars that distorted the palms of his hands. What had happened? A fishing accident?

Quickly she averted her eyes so he wouldn't notice her shock. Or see the questions she didn't dare ask.

Not now. Not yet.

She rushed to fill the silence that had fallen over their table. 'It's been a—'

He finished the sentence for her. 'Long time?'

'Yes,' was all she was able to get out. 'I was only thinking about you a minute ago and wondering...'

She felt the colour rise up her throat to stain her cheeks. As she'd walked away from the information kiosk and towards the hotel hadn't she been remembering how Ben had kissed her all those years ago, as they'd lain entwined on the sand in the shadows at the back of the Morgan family's boat shed? Remembering the promises they'd made to each other between those breathless kisses? Promises she'd really, truly believed.

She felt again as gauche and awkward as she had the night she'd first danced with him, at a bushfire brigade fundraiser dance at the surf club a lifetime ago. Unable to believe that Ben Morgan had actually singled her out from the summer people who'd invaded the locals' dance.

After their second dance together he'd asked her if she had a boyfriend back home. When she'd shaken her head, he'd smiled.

'Good,' he'd said. 'Then I don't have to go up to Sydney and fight him for you.'

She'd been so thrilled she'd actually felt dizzy.

The waiter arrived at their table.

'Can I get you another drink?' Ben asked.

'Um, diet cola, please.'

What was wrong with her? Why was she so jittery and on edge?

As a teenager she'd always felt relaxed with Ben, able to be herself. She'd gone home to Sydney a different person from the one who had arrived for that two-week holiday in Dolphin Bay.

She had to stop being so uptight. This was the same Ben. Older, but still Ben. He seemed the same laid-back guy he'd been as her teenage heartthrob.

Except—she suppressed a shudder—for the horrendous scarring on his hands.

'Would you believe this is the first time I've been back this way since that summer?' she said, looking straight into his eyes. She'd used to tell him that eyes so blue were wasted on a man and beg him to swap them for her ordinary hazel-brownish ones.

'It's certainly the first time I've seen you here,' he said easily.

Was he, too, remembering those laughing intimacies they'd once shared? Those long discussions of what they'd do with their lives, full of hopes and dreams and youthful optimism? Their resolve not to let the distance between Dolphin Bay and Sydney stop them from seeing each other again?

If he was, he certainly didn't show it. 'So what brings you back?' he asked.

It seemed a polite, uninterested question—the kind a long-ago acquaintance might ask a scarcely remembered stranger who'd blown unexpectedly into town.

'The sun, the surf and the dolphins?' she said, determined to match his tone.

He smiled. 'The surf's as good as it always was, and the dolphins are still here. But there must be something else to bring a city girl like you to this particular backwater.'

'B…backwater? I wouldn't call it that,' she stuttered. 'I'm sorry if you think I—' The gleam in his blue eyes told her he wasn't serious. She recovered herself. 'I'm on my way from Sydney through to Melbourne. I saw the turn to this wonderful non-backwater town and here I am. On impulse.'

'It's nice you decided to drop in.' His words were casual, just the right thing to say. Almost too casual. 'So, how do you find the place?'

She'd never had to lie with Ben. Still, she was in the habit of being tactful. And this *was* Ben's hometown.

'I can't tell you how overjoyed I was to see those dolphin rubbish bins still there.'

Ben laughed, his strong, even teeth very white against his tan.

That laugh. It still had the power to warm her. Her heart did a curious flipping over thing as she remembered all the laughter they'd shared that long-ago summer. No wonder she'd recognised it instantly.

'Those hellish things,' he said. 'There's always someone on the progress association who wants to rip them out, but they're always shouted down.'

'Thank heaven for that,' she said. 'It wouldn't be Dolphin Bay without them.'

'People have even started a rumour that if the dolphins are removed it will be the end of Dolphin Bay.'

She giggled. 'Seriously?'

'Seriously,' he said, straight-faced. 'The rubbish bins go and as punishment we'll be struck by a tsunami. Or some other calamity.'

He rolled his eyes. Just like he'd used to do. That

hidden part of her heart marked 'first love' reacted with a painful lurch. She averted her gaze from his mouth and that intriguing, sexy little scar.

She remembered the hours of surfing with him, playing tennis on that old court out at the back of the guesthouse. The fun. The laughter. Those passionate, heartfelt kisses. Oh, those kisses—his mouth hard and warm and exciting on hers, his tongue exploring, teasing. Her body straining to his…

The memories gave her the courage to ask the question. It was now or never. 'Ben. It was a long time ago. But…but why didn't you write like you said you would?'

For a long moment he didn't answer and she tensed. Then he shrugged. 'I never was much for letters. After you didn't answer the first two I didn't bother again.'

An edge to his voice hinted that his words weren't as carefree as they seemed. She shook her head in disbelief. 'You wrote me two letters?'

'The day after you went home. Then the week after that. Like I promised to.'

Her mouth went suddenly dry. 'I never got a letter. Never. Or a phone call. I always wondered why…'

No way would she admit how, day after day, she'd hung around the letterbox, hoping against hope that he'd write. Her strict upbringing had meant she was very short on dating experience and vulnerable to doubt.

'Don't chase after boys,' her mother had told her,

over and over again. *'Men are hunters. If he's interested he'll come after you. If he doesn't you'll only make a fool of yourself by throwing yourself at him.'*

But in spite of her mother's advice she'd tried to phone Ben. Three times she'd braved a phone call to the guesthouse but had hung up without identifying herself when his father had answered. On the third time his father had told her not to ring again. Had he thought she was a nuisance caller? Or realised it was her and didn't want her bothering his son? Her eighteen-year-old self had assumed the latter.

It had been humiliating. Too humiliating to admit it even now to Ben.

'Your dad probably got to my letters before you could,' said Ben. 'He never approved of me.'

'That's not true,' Sandy stated half-heartedly, knowing she wouldn't put it past her controlling, righteous father to have intercepted any communication from Ben. In fact she and Ben had decided it was best he not phone her because of her father's disapproval of the relationship.

'He's just a small-town Lothario, Alexandra.' Her father's long-ago words echoed in her head. Hardly. Ben had treated her with the utmost respect. Unlike the private school sons of his friends her father had tried to foist on her.

'Your dad wanted more for you than a small-town fisherman.' Ben's blue eyes were shrewd and piercing. 'And you probably came to agree with him.'

Sandy dropped her gaze and shifted uncomfortably in her seat. Over and over her father had told her to forget about Ben. He wasn't suitable. They came from different worlds. Where was the future for a girl who had academic talents like hers with a boy who'd finished high school but had no intention of going any further?

Underneath it all had been the unspoken message: *He's not good enough for you.*

She'd never believed that—not for a second. But she had come to believe there was no future for them.

Inconsolable after their summer together, she'd sobbed into her pillow at night when Ben hadn't written. Scribbled endless notes to him she'd never had the courage to send.

But he hadn't got in touch and she'd forced herself to forget him. To get over something that obviously hadn't meant anything to him.

'Men make promises they never intend to keep, Alexandra.' How many times had her mother told her that?

Then, once she'd started university in Sydney, Dolphin Bay and Ben Morgan had seemed far away and less and less important. Her father was right— a surfer boyfriend wouldn't have fitted in with her new crowd anyway, she'd told herself. Then there'd been other boys. Other kisses. And she'd been too grown up for family holidays at Dolphin Bay or anywhere else.

Still, there remained a place in her heart that had

always stayed a little raw, that hurt if she pulled out her memories and prodded at them.

But Ben had written to her.

She swirled the ice cubes round and round in her glass, still unable to meet his eyes, not wanting him to guess how disconcerted she felt. How the knowledge he hadn't abandoned her teenage self took the sting from her memories.

'It was a long time ago…' she repeated, her voice tapering away. 'Things change.'

'Yep. Twelve years tends to do that.'

She wasn't sure if he was talking about her, him, or the town. She seized on the more neutral option.

'Yes.' She looked around her, waved a hand to encompass the stark fashionable furnishings. 'Like this hotel.'

'What about this hotel?'

'It's very smart, but not very sympathetic, is it?'

'I kinda like it myself,' he said, and took a drink from his beer.

'You're not upset at what the developers did on the site of your family's beautiful guesthouse?'

'Like you said. Things change. The guesthouse has…has gone forever.'

He paused and she got the impression he had to control his voice.

'But this hotel and all the new developments around it have brought jobs for a lot of people. Some say it's the best thing that's ever happened to the place.'

'Do you?'

Sandy willed him to say no, wanting Ben to be the same carefree boy who'd lived for the next good wave, the next catch from the fishing boats he'd shared with his father, but knew somehow from the expression on his face that he wouldn't.

But still his reply came as a surprise. 'I own this hotel, Sandy.'

'You…you do?'

'Yep. Unsympathetic design and all.'

She clapped her hand to her mouth but she couldn't take back the words. 'I'm…I'm so sorry I insulted it.'

'No offence taken on behalf of the award-winning architect.'

'Really? It's won awards?'

'A stack of 'em.'

She noted the convivial atmosphere at the bar, the rapidly filling tables. 'It's very smart, of course. And I'm sure it's very successful. It's just…the old place was so charming. Your mother was so proud of it.'

'My parents left the guesthouse long ago. Glad to say goodbye to the erratic plumbing and the creaking floorboards. They built themselves a comfortable new house up on the headland when I took over.'

Whoa. Surprise on surprise. She knew lots must have changed in twelve years, but this? 'You took over the running of the guesthouse?' Somehow, she couldn't see Ben in that role. She thought of him always as outdoors, an action man—not indoors, pandering to the whims of guests.

'My wife did.'

His wife.

The words stabbed into Sandy's heart.

His wife.

If she hadn't already been sitting down she would have had to. Stupidly, she hadn't considered—not for one minute—that Ben would be married.

She shot a quick glance at his left hand. He didn't wear a wedding ring, but then plenty of married men didn't. She'd learned that lesson since she'd been single again.

'Of course. Of course you would have married,' she babbled, forcing her mouth into the semblance of a smile.

She clutched her glass so tightly she feared it would shatter. Frantically she tried to mould her expression into something normal, show a polite interest in an old friend's new life.

'Did you…did you marry someone from around here?'

'Jodi Hart.'

Immediately Sandy remembered her. Jodi, with her quiet manner and gentle heart-shaped face. 'She was lovely,' she said, meaning every word while trying not to let an unwarranted jealousy flame into life.

'Yes,' Ben said, and a muscle pulled at the side of his mouth, giving it a weary twist.

His face seemed suddenly drawn under the bronze of his tan. She was aware of lines etched around his features. She hadn't noticed them in the first flush of surprise at their meeting. Maybe their marriage wasn't happy.

Ben drummed his fingers on the surface of the table. Again her eyes were drawn to the scars on his hands. Horrible, angry ridges that made her wince at the sight of them.

'What about you?' he asked. 'Did you marry?'

Sandy shook her head. 'Me? Marry? No. My partner…he…he didn't believe in marriage.'

Her voice sounded brittle to her own ears. How she'd always hated that ambiguous term *partner*.

'"Just a piece of paper," he used to say.' She forced a laugh and hoped it concealed any trace of heartbreak. 'Sure made it easy when we split up. No messy divorce or anything.'

No way would she admit how distraught she'd been. How angry and hurt and humiliated.

His jaw clenched. 'I'm sorry. Did—?'

She put her hand up to stop his words. 'Thank you. But there's no point in talking about it.' She made herself smile. 'Water under the bridge, you know.'

It was six months since she'd last seen Jason. And that had only been to pay him for his half of the sofa they'd bought together.

Ben looked at her as if he were searching her face for something. His gaze was so intense she began to feel uncomfortable. When—at last—he spoke, his words were slow and considered.

'Water under the bridge. You're right.'

'Yes,' she said, not sure what to say next.

After another long, awkward pause, he glanced at his watch. 'It's been great to see you, Sandy. But I have a meeting to get to.' He pushed back his chair and got up.

'Of course.' She wanted to put out a hand to stop him. There was more she wanted to ask him. Memories she wanted to share. But there was no reason for him to stay. No reason for him to know it was her birthday and how much she would enjoy his company for lunch.

He was married.

Married men did not share intimate lunches alone with former girlfriends, even if their last kiss had been twelve years ago.

She got up, too, resisting the urge to sigh. 'It was wonderful to catch up after all these years. Please… please give my regards to Jodi.'

He nodded, not meeting her eyes. Then indicated the menu. 'Lunch is on the house. I'll tell the desk you're my guest.'

'You really don't have to, Ben.'

'Please. I insist. For…for old times' sake.'

She hesitated. Then smiled tentatively. 'Okay. Thank you. I'm being nostalgic but they were good old times, weren't they? I have only happy memories of Dolphin Bay.' *Of the time we spent together.*

She couldn't kiss him goodbye. Instead she offered her hand for him to shake.

He paused for a second, then took it in his warm grip, igniting memories of the feel of his hands on her body, the caresses that had never gone further than she'd wanted. But back then she hadn't felt the hard ridges of those awful scars. And now she had no right to recall such intimate memories.

Ben was married.

'I'm sorry I was rude about your hotel,' she said, very seriously. Then she injected a teasing tone into her voice. 'But I'll probably never stop wondering why you destroyed the guesthouse. And those magnificent gum trees—there's not one left. Remember the swing that—?'

Ben let go her hand. 'Sandy. It was just a building.'

Too late she realised it wasn't any of her business to go on about the guesthouse just because she was disappointed it had been demolished.

'Ben, I—'

He cut across her. 'It's fine. That was the past, and it's where it should be. But it really has been great seeing you again…enjoy your lunch. Goodbye, Sandy.'

'Good-goodbye, Ben,' she managed to stutter out, stunned by his abrupt farewell, by the feeling that he wasn't being completely honest with her.

Without another word he turned from her, strode to the exit, nodded towards the people at the bar, and closed the door behind him. She gripped the edge of the table, swept by a wave of disappointment so intense she felt she was drowning in it.

What had she said? Had she crossed a line without knowing it? And why did she feel emptier than when she'd first arrived back in Dolphin Bay? Because when she'd written her birthday resolutions hadn't she had Ben Morgan in mind? When she'd described a kind man, free of hang-ups and deadly ambition, hadn't she been remembering him? Remembering how his straightforward approach to life had helped her grow up that summer? Grow up enough to defy her father and set her own course.

She was forced to admit to herself it wasn't the pier or the guesthouse she'd wanted to be the same in Dolphin Bay. It was the man who represented the antithesis of the cruel, city-smart man who had hurt her so badly.

In her self-centred fantasy she hadn't given a thought to Ben being married—just to him always being here, stuck in a time warp.

A waitress appeared to clear her glass away, but then paused and looked at her. Sandy wished she'd put her sunglasses back on. Her hurt, her disappointment, her anger at herself, must be etched on her face.

The waitress was a woman of about her own age, with a pretty freckled face and curly auburn hair pulled back tightly. Her eyes narrowed. 'I know you,' she said suddenly. 'Sandy, right? Years ago you came down from Sydney to stay at Morgan's Guesthouse.'

'That's right,' Sandy said, taken aback at being recognised.

'I'm Kate Parker,' the woman said, 'but I don't suppose you remember me.'

Sandy dredged through her memories. 'Yes, I do.' She forced a smile. 'You were the best dancer I'd ever seen. My sister and I desperately tried to copy you, but we could never be as good.'

'Thanks,' Kate replied, looking pleased at the compliment. She looked towards the door Ben had exited through. 'You dated Ben, didn't you? Poor guy. He's had it tough.'

'Tough?'

'You don't know?' The other woman's voice was almost accusing.

How would she know what had gone on in Ben Morgan's life in the twelve years since she'd last seen him?

'Lost his wife and child when the old guesthouse burned down,' Kate continued. 'Jodi died trying to rescue their little boy. Ben was devastated. Went away for a long time—did very well for himself. When he came back he built this hotel as modern and as different from the old place as could be. Couldn't bear the memories…'

Kate Parker chattered on, but Sandy didn't wait to hear any more. She pushed her chair back so fast it fell over and clattered onto the ground. She didn't stop to pull it up.

She ran out of the bar, through the door and to-wards the steps to the shoreline, heart pumping, face flushed, praying frantically to the god of second chances.

Ben.

She just had to find Ben.

CHAPTER TWO

TAKING THE STEPS two at a time, nearly tripping over her feet in her haste, Sandy ran onto the whiter-than-white sand of Dolphin Bay.

Ben was way ahead of her. Tall and broad-shouldered, he strode along towards the rocks, defying the wind that had sprung up while she was in the hotel and was now whipping the water to a frosting of whitecaps.

She had to catch up with him. Explain. Apologise. Tell him how dreadfully sorry she was about Jodi and his son. Tell him… Oh, so much she wanted to tell him. Needed to tell him. But the deep, fine sand was heavy around her feet, slowing her so she felt she was making no progress at all.

'Ben!' she shouted, but the wind just snatched the words out of her mouth and he didn't turn around.

She fumbled with her sandals and yanked them off, the better to run after him.

'Ben!' she called again, her voice hoarse, the salt wind whipping her hair around her face and stinging her eyes.

At last he stopped. Slowly, warily, he turned to face her. It seemed an age until she'd struggled through the sand to reach him. He stood unmoving, his face rigid, his eyes guarded. How hadn't she seen it before?

'Ben,' she whispered, scarcely able to get the word out. 'I'm sorry… I can't tell you how sorry I am.'

His eyes searched her face. 'You know?'

She nodded. 'Kate told me. She thought I already knew. I don't know what to say.'

Ben looked down at Sandy's face, at her cheeks flushed pink, her brown hair all tangled and blown around her face. Her eyes were huge with distress, her mouth oddly stained bright pink in the centre. She didn't look much older than the girl he'd loved all those years ago.

The girl he'd recognised as soon as she'd come into the hotel restaurant. Recognised and—just for one wild, unguarded second before he pummelled the thought back down to the depths of his wounded heart—let himself exult that she had come back. His first love. The girl he had never forgotten. Had never expected to see again.

For just those few minutes when they'd chatted he'd donned the mask of the carefree boy he'd been when they'd last met.

'I'm so sorry,' she said again, her voice barely audible through the wind.

'You couldn't have known,' he said.

Silence fell between them for a long moment and he found he could not stop himself from searching her face. Looking for change. He wanted there to be no sign of the passing years on her, though he was aware of how much he had changed himself.

Then she spoke. 'When did…?'

'Five years ago,' he said gruffly.

He didn't want to talk to Sandy about what the locals called 'his tragedy'. He didn't want to talk about it anymore full-stop—but particularly not to Sandy, who'd once been so special to him.

Sandy Adams belonged in his past. Firmly in his past. *Water under the bridge*, as she'd so aptly said.

She bit down on her lower lip. 'I can't imagine how you must feel—'

'No, you can't,' he said, more abruptly than he'd intended, and was ashamed at the flash of hurt that tightened her face. 'No one could. But I've put it behind me…'

Her eyes—warm, compassionate—told him she knew he was lying. How could he ever put that terrible day of helpless rage and despair behind him? The empty, guilt-ridden days that had followed it? The years of punishing himself, of not allowing himself to feel again?

'Your hands,' she said softly. 'Is that how you hurt them?'

He nodded, finding words with difficulty. 'The metal door handles were burning hot when I tried to open them.'

Fearsome images came back—the heat, the smoke, the door that would not give despite his weight behind it, his voice raw from screaming Jodi's and Liam's names.

He couldn't stop the shudder that racked his frame. 'I don't talk about it.'

Mutely, she nodded, and her eyes dropped from his face. But not before he read the sorrow for him there.

Once again he felt ashamed of his harshness towards her. But that was him these days. Ben Morgan: thirty-one going on ninety.

His carefree self of that long-ago summer had been forged into someone tougher, harder, colder. Someone who would not allow emotion or softness in his life. Even the memories of a holiday romance. For with love came the agony of loss, and he could never risk that again.

She looked up at him. 'If…if there's anything I can do to help, you'll let me know, won't you?'

Again he nodded, but knew in his heart it was an empty gesture. Sandy was just passing through, and he was grateful. He didn't want to revisit times past.

He'd only loved two women—his wife, Jodi, and, before her, Sandy. It was too dangerous to have his first love around, reminding him of what he'd vowed never to feel again. He'd resigned himself to a life alone.

'You've booked in to the hotel?' he asked.

'Not yet, but I will.'

'For how long?'

Visibly, her face relaxed. She was obviously relieved at the change of subject. He remembered she'd never been very good at hiding her emotions.

'Just tonight,' she said. 'I'm on my way to Melbourne for an interview about a franchise opportunity.'

'Why Melbourne?' That was a hell of a long way from Dolphin Bay—as he knew from his years at university there.

'Why not?' she countered.

He turned and started walking towards the rocks again. Automatically she fell into step behind him. He waited.

Yes. He wasn't imagining it. It was happening.

After every three of his long strides she had to skip for a bit to keep up with him. Just like she had twelve years ago. And she didn't even seem to be aware that she was doing it.

'You're happy to leave Sydney?'

'There's nothing for me in Sydney now,' she replied.

Her voice was light, matter-of-fact, but he didn't miss the underlying note of bitterness.

He stopped. Went to halt her with a hand on her arm and thought better of it. No matter. She automatically stopped with him, in tune with the rhythm of his pace.

'Nothing?' he asked.

Not meeting his gaze, swinging her sandals by

her side, she shrugged. 'Well, my sister Lizzie and my niece Amy. But…no one else.'

'Your parents?'

Her mouth twisted in spite of her effort to smile. 'They're not together any more. Turns out Dad had been cheating on my mother for years. The first Mum heard about it was when his mistress contacted her, soon after we got home from Dolphin Bay that summer. He and Mum patched it up that time. And the next. Finally he left her for his receptionist. She's two years older than I am.'

'I'm sorry to hear that.'

But he was not surprised. He'd never liked the self-righteous Dr Randall Adams. Had hated the way he'd tried to control every aspect of Sandy's life. He wasn't surprised the older man had intercepted his long-ago letters. He'd made it very clear he had considered a fisherman not good enough for a doctor's daughter.

'That must have been difficult for you,' he said.

Sandy pushed her windblown hair back from her face in a gesture he remembered. 'I'm okay about it. Now. And Mum's remarried to a very nice man and living in Queensland.'

During that summer he'd used to tease her about her optimism. 'You should be called Sunny, not Sandy,' he'd say as he kissed the tip of her sunburned nose. 'You never let anything get you down.'

It seemed she hadn't changed—in that regard anyway. But when he looked closely at her face he could see a tightness around her mouth, a wariness in her eyes he didn't recall.

Maybe things weren't always so sunny for her these days. Perhaps her cup-half-full mentality had been challenged by life's storm clouds in the twelve years since he'd last seen her.

Suddenly she glanced at her watch. She couldn't smother her gasp. The colour drained from her face.

'What's wrong?' he asked immediately.

'Nothing,' she said, tight lipped.

Nothing. Why did women always say that when something was clearly wrong?

'Then why did you stare at your watch like it was about to explode? Is it connected to a bomb somewhere?'

That brought a twitch to her lips. 'I wish.'

She lifted her eyes from the watch. Her gaze was steady. 'I don't know why I'm telling you this, but right at this very moment Jason—my...my former boyfriend, partner, live-in lover or whatever you like to call him—is getting married.'

Sandy with a live-in boyfriend? She'd said she'd had a partner but had it been that serious? The knowledge hit him in the gut. Painfully. Unexpectedly. Stupidly.

What he and Sandy had had together was a teen romance. Kid stuff. They'd both moved on. He'd married Jodi. Of course Sandy would have had another man in her life.

But he had to clear his throat to reply. 'And that's bad or good?'

She laughed. But the laugh didn't quite reach her eyes. 'Well, good for him. Good for her, I guess. I'm still not sure how I feel about coming home one day to find his possessions gone and a note telling me he'd moved in with her.'

'You're kidding me, right?' Ben growled. How could someone treat his Sandy like that. *His Sandy.* That was a slip. She hadn't been his for a long, long time.

'I'm afraid not. It was…humiliating to say the least.' Her tone sounded forced, light. 'But, hey, it makes for a great story.'

A great story? Yeah, right.

There went sunny Sandy again, laughing off something that must still cause her pain.

'Sounds to me like you're better off without him.'

'The further I get from him the more I can see that,' she said. But she didn't sound convinced.

'As far away as Melbourne?' he asked, finding the thought of her so far away unsettling.

'I'm not running away,' she said firmly. Too firmly. 'I need change. A new job, a new—'

'Your job? What is that?' he asked, realising how little he knew about her now. 'Did you study law like your father wanted?'

'No, I didn't. Don't look so surprised—it was because of you.'

'Me?' No wonder her father had hated him.

'You urged me to follow my dreams—like you were following yours. I thought about that a lot when I got back home. And my dream wasn't to be a solicitor.' She shuddered. 'I couldn't think of anything less me.'

He'd studied law as part of his degree and liked it. But he wasn't as creative as he remembered Sandy being. 'But you studied for years so you'd get a place in law.'

'Law at Sydney University.' She pronounced the words as though they were spelled in capital letters. 'That was my father's ambition for me. He'd given up his plans for me to be a doctor when I didn't cut it in chemistry.'

'You didn't get enough marks in the Higher School Certificate for law?'

'I got the marks, all right. Not long after we got back to Sydney the results came out. I was in the honour roll in the newspaper. You should have heard my father boasting to anyone who'd listen to him.'

'I'll bet he did.' Ben had no respect for the guy. He was a bully and a snob. But he had reason to be grateful to him. Not for ruining things with him and Sandy. But for putting the bomb under him he'd needed to get off his teenage butt and make himself worthy of a girl like Sandy.

'At the last minute I switched to a communications degree. At what my father considered a lesser university.'

'He must have hit the roof.'

Sandy's mouth tightened to a thin line. 'As he'd just been outed as an adulterer he didn't have a leg to stand on about doing the right thing for the family.'

Ben smiled. It sounded as if Sandy had got a whole lot feistier when it came to standing up to her father. 'So what career did you end up in?'

'I'm in advertising.' She quickly corrected herself. 'I *was* in advertising. An account executive.'

On occasion he dealt with an advertising agency to help promote his hotel. The account executives were slick, efficient, and tough as old boots. Not at all the way he thought of Sandy. 'Sounds impressive.'

'It was.'

'Was?'

'Long story,' she said, and started to walk towards the rocks again.

'I'm listening,' he said, falling into step beside her.

The wind had dropped and now the air around them seemed unnaturally still. Seagulls screeched raucously. He looked through narrowed eyes to the horizon, where grey clouds were banking up ominously.

Sandy followed his gaze. She wrinkled her cute up-tilted nose. 'Storm brewing,' she said. 'I wonder—'

'Don't change the subject by talking about the weather,' he said, stopping himself from adding, *I remember how you always did that.*

He shouldn't have let himself get reeled in to

such a nostalgic conversation. There was no point in dredging up those old memories. Not when their lives were now set on such different paths. And his path was one he needed—wanted—to tread unencumbered. He could not survive more loss. And the best way to avoid loss was to avoid the kind of attachment that could tear a man apart.

He wanted to spend his life alone. Though the word 'alone' seemed today to have a desolate echo to it.

She shrugged. 'Okay. Back to my story. Jason and I were both working at the same agency when we met. The boss didn't think it was a good idea when we started dating…'

'So you had to go? Not him?'

She pulled a face. 'We…ell. I convinced myself I'd been there long enough.'

'So you went elsewhere? Another agency?'

She nodded. 'And then the economy hit a blip, advertising revenues suffered, and last one in was first one out.'

'That must have been tough.'

'Yeah. It was. But, hey, one door closes and another one opens, right? I got freelance work at different agencies and learned a whole lot of stuff I might never have known otherwise.'

Yep, that was the old Sandy all right—never one to allow adversity to cloud her spirit.

She took a deep breath. He noticed how her breasts rose under her tight-fitting top. She'd filled out—womanly curves softened the angles of her teenage body. Her face was subtly different too, her cheekbones more defined, her mouth fuller.

He wouldn't have thought it possible but she was even more beautiful than she'd been when she was eighteen.

He wrenched his gaze away, cleared his throat. 'So you're looking at a franchise?'

Her eyes sparkled and her voice rose with excitement. 'My chance to be my own boss, run my own show. It's this awesome candle store. A former client of mine started it.'

'You were in advertising and now you want to sell candles? Aren't there enough candle stores in this world?'

'These aren't ordinary candles, Ben. The store is a raging success in Sydney. Now they're looking to open up in other towns. They're interviewing for a Melbourne franchise and I put my hand up.'

She paused.

'I want to do something different. Something of my own. Something challenging.'

She looked so earnest, so determined, that he couldn't help a teasing note from entering his voice. 'So it's candles? I don't see the challenge there.'

'Don't you?' she asked. 'There's a scented candle for every mood, you know—to relax, to stimulate, to seduce—'

She stopped on the last word, and the colour deepened in her cheeks, flushed the creamy skin of her neck. Her eyelashes fluttered nervously and she couldn't meet his gaze.

'Well, you get the story. I wrote the copy for the client. There's not much I don't know about the merits of those candles.' She was almost gabbling now to cover her embarrassment.

To seduce.

When he'd been nineteen, seducing Sandy had been all he'd thought about. Until he'd fallen in love with her. Then respecting her innocence had become more important than his own desires. The number of cold showers he'd been forced to take…

Thunder rumbled ominously over the water. 'C'mon,' he said gruffly, 'we'd better turn back.'

'Yes,' she said. 'Though I suppose it's too late now for my birthday lunch…' She hesitated. 'Please—forget I just said that, will you?'

'It's your birthday today?'

She shrugged dismissively. 'Yes. It's nothing special.'

He thought back. 'It's your *thirtieth* birthday.'

And she was celebrating alone?

'Eek,' she said in an exaggerated tone. 'Please don't remind me of my advancing years.'

'February—of course. How could I forget?' he said slowly.

'You remember my birthday?'

'I'd be lying if I said I recalled the exact date. But I remember it was in February because you were always pointing out how compatible our star signs were. Remember you used to check our horoscopes in your father's newspaper every day and—?'

He checked himself. Mentally he slammed his hand against his forehead. He'd been so determined not to indulge in reminiscence about that summer and now he'd gone and started it himself.

She didn't seem to notice his sudden reticence. 'Yes, I remember. You're Leo and I'm Pisces,' she chattered on. 'And you always gave me a hard time about it. Said astrology was complete hokum and the people at the newspaper just made the horoscopes up.'

'I still think that and—' He stopped as a loud clap of thunder drowned out his voice. Big, cold drops of water started pelting his head.

Sandy laughed. 'The heavens are angry at you for mocking them.'

'Sure,' he said, but found himself unable to resist a smile at her whimsy. 'And if you don't want to get drenched we've got to make a run for it.'

'Race you!' she challenged, still laughing, and took off, her slim, tanned legs flashing ahead of him.

He caught up with her in just a few strides.

'Not fair,' she said, panting a little. 'Your legs are longer than mine.'

He slowed his pace just enough so she wouldn't think he was purposely letting her win.

She glanced up at him as they ran side by side, her eyes lively with laughter, fat drops of water dampening her hair and rolling down her flushed cheeks.

The sight of her vivacity ignited something deep inside him—something long dormant, like a piece of machinery, seized and unwanted, suddenly grinding slowly to life.

'I gave you a head start,' he managed to choke out in reply to her complaint.

But he didn't get a chance to say anything else for, waiting at the top of the stairs to the hotel, wringing her hands anxiously together, stood Kate Parker.

'Oh, Ben, thank heaven. I didn't know where you were. Your aunt Ida has had a fall and hurt her pelvis, but she won't let the ambulance take her to hospital until she's spoken to you.'

CHAPTER THREE

SANDY WAS HALFWAY up the stairs, determined to beat Ben to the top. Slightly out of breath, she couldn't help smiling to herself over the fact that Ben had remembered her birthday. Hmm... Should she be reading something into that?

And then Kate was there, with her worried expression and urgent words, and the smile froze on Sandy's face.

She immediately looked to Ben. Her heart seemed to miss a beat as his face went rigid, every trace of laughter extinguished.

'What happened?' he demanded of the red-haired waitress.

'She fell—'

'Tap-dancing? Or playing tennis?'

Kate's face was pale under her freckles. 'Neither. Ida fell moving a pile of books. You know what she's like. Pretends she's thirty-five, not seventy-five—'

Ida? A seventy-five-year-old tap-dancing aunt? Sandy vaguely remembered Ben all those years ago talking about an aunt—a great-aunt?—he'd adored.

'Where is she?' Ben growled, oblivious to the rain falling down on him in slow, heavy drops, slicking his hair, dampening his shirt so it clung to his back and shoulders, defining his powerful muscles.

'In the ambulance in front of her bookshop,' said Kate. 'Better hurry. I'll tell the staff where you are, then join you—'

Before Kate had finished speaking, Ben had turned on his heel and headed around to the side of the hotel with the long, athletic strides Sandy had always had trouble keeping up with.

'Ben!' Sandy called after him, then forced herself to stop. Wasn't this her cue to cut out? As in, *Goodbye, Ben, it was cool to catch up with you. Best of luck with everything. See ya.*

That would be the sensible option. And Sandy, the practical list-maker, might be advised to take it. Sandy, who was on her way to Melbourne and a new career. A new life.

But this was about Ben.

Ben, with his scarred hands and scarred heart.

Ben, who might need some support.

Whether he wanted it or not.

'I'm coming with you,' she called after him, all thoughts of her thirtieth birthday lunch put on hold.

Quickly she fastened the buckles on her sandals. Wished for a moment that she had an umbrella. But she didn't really care about getting wet. She just wanted to be with Ben.

She'd never met a more masculine man, but the

tragedy he had suffered gave him a vulnerability she could not ignore. Was he in danger of losing someone else he loved? It was an unbearable thought.

'Ben! Wait for me!' she called.

He turned and glanced back at her, but made no comment as she caught up with him. Good, so he didn't mind her tagging along.

His hand brushed hers as they strode along together. She longed to take it and squeeze it reassuringly but didn't dare. Touching wasn't on the agenda. Not any more.

Within minutes they'd reached the row of new shops that ran down from the side of the hotel.

There was an ambulance parked on the footpath out of the rain, under the awning in front of a shop named Bay Books. When she'd driven past she'd admired it because of its charming doorframe, carved with frolicking dolphins. Who'd have thought she'd next be looking at it under circumstances like this?

A slight, elderly lady with cropped silver hair lay propped up on a gurney in front of the open ambulance doors.

This was Great-Aunt Ida?

Sandy scoured her memories. Twelve years ago she'd been so in love with Ben she'd lapped up any detail about his family, anything that concerned him. Wasn't there a story connected to Ida? Something the family had had to live down?

Ben was instantly by his aunt's side. 'Idy, what

have you done to yourself this time?' he scolded, in a stern but loving voice.

He gripped Ida's fragile gnarled hand with his much bigger, scarred one. Sandy caught her breath at the look of exasperated tenderness on his face. Remembered how caring he'd been to the people he loved. How protective he'd been of *her* when she was eighteen.

Back then she'd been so scared of the big waves. Every day Ben had coaxed her a little further from the shore, building her confidence with his reassuring presence. On the day she'd finally caught a wave and ridden her body-board all the way in to shore, squealing and laughing at the exhilaration of it, she'd looked back to see he had arranged an escort of his brother and his best mates—all riding the same break. What kind of guy would do that? She'd never met one since, that was for sure.

'Cracked my darn pelvis, they think. I tripped, that's all.' Ida's face was contorted with annoyance as much as with pain.

Ben whipped around to face the ambulance officer standing by his aunt. 'Then why isn't she in the hospital?'

'Point-blank refused to let me take her. Insisted on seeing you first,' the paramedic said with raised eyebrows and admirable restraint, considering the way Ben was glaring at him. 'Tried to get her to call you from hospital but she wasn't budging.'

'That's right,' said Ben's aunt in a surprisingly

strong voice. 'I'm not going anywhere until my fa-vourite great-nephew promises to look after my shop.'

'Absolutely,' said Ben, without a second's hesita-tion. 'I'll lock it up safely. Now, c'mon, let's get you in the ambulance and—'

His aunt Ida tried to rise from the gurney. 'That's not what I meant. That's not good enough—' she said, before her words were cut short by a little whimper of pain.

Sandy shifted from sodden sandal to sodden san-dal. Looked away to the intricately carved awning. She felt like an interloper, an uninvited witness to Ben's intimate family drama. Why hadn't she stayed at the beach?

'Don't worry about the shop,' said Ben, his voice burred with worry. 'I'll sort something out for you. Let's just get you to the hospital.'

'It's not life or death,' said the paramedic, 'but, yes, she should be on her way.'

Ida closed her eyes briefly and Sandy's heart lurched at the weariness that crossed her face. *Please let her be all right—for Ben's sake.*

But then the older lady's eyes snapped into life again. They were the same blue as Ben's and re-markably unfaded. 'I can't leave my shop closed for all that time.'

The paramedic interrupted. 'She might have to lie still in bed for weeks.'

'That's not acceptable,' continued the formidable

Ida. 'You'll have to find me a manager. Keep my business going.'

'Just get to the ER and I'll do something about that later,' said Ben.

'Not later. *Now*,' said Aunt Ida, sounding nothing like a little old lady lying seriously injured on a gurney. Maybe she was pumped full of painkillers.

Sandy struggled to suppress a grin. For all his tough, grown-up ways she could still see the nineteen-year-old Ben. He was obviously aching to bundle his feisty aunt into the ambulance but was too respectful to try it.

Aunt Ida's eyes sought out Kate, who was now standing next to Sandy. 'Kate? Can you—?'

Kate shook her head regretfully. 'No can do, I'm afraid.'

'She's needed at the hotel. We're short-staffed,' said Ben, with an edge of impatience to his voice.

Ida's piercing blue gaze turned to Sandy. 'What about you?'

'Me?' Was the old lady serious? Or delirious?

Before Sandy could stutter out anything more, Kate had turned to face her.

Her eyes narrowed. 'Yes. What about you, Sandy? Are you on holiday? Could you help out?'

'What? No. Sorry. I'm on my way to Melbourne.' She was so aghast she was gabbling. 'I'm afraid I won't be able to—'

'Friend of Kate's, are you?' persisted the old lady,

in a voice that in spite of her obvious efforts was beginning to tire.

Compelled by good manners, Sandy took a step forward. 'No. Yes. Kind of… I—'

She looked imploringly at Ben, uncertain of what to say, not wanting to make an already difficult situation worse.

'Sandy's an…an old friend of mine,' he said, stumbling on the word friend. 'Just passing through.'

'Oh,' said the older lady, 'so she can't help out. And I can't afford to lose even a day's business.'

Her face seemed to collapse and she looked every minute of her seventy-five years.

Suddenly she reminded Sandy of her grandmother—her mother's mother. How would she feel if Grandma were stuck in a situation like this?

'I'm sorry,' she said reluctantly.

'Pity.' Ida sighed. 'You look nice. Intelligent. The kind of person I could trust with my shop.' Wearily she closed her eyes again. 'Find me someone like her, Ben.'

Her voice was beginning to waver. Sandy could barely hear it over the sound of the rain drumming on the awning overhead.

Ben looked from Sandy to his aunt and then back to Sandy again, his eyes unreadable. 'Maybe… maybe Sandy can be convinced to stay for a few days,' he said.

Huh? Sandy stared at him. 'But, Ben, I—'

Ben held her with his glance, his blue eyes intense. He leaned closer to her. 'Just play along with me and say yes so I can get her to go to the hospital,' he muttered from the side of his mouth.

'Oh.' She paused. Thought for a moment. Thought again. 'Okay. I'll look after the shop. Just for a few days. Until you get someone else.'

'You promise?' asked Ida.

Promise? Like a cross-your-heart-and-hope-to-die-type promise? The kind of promise she never went back on?

Disconcerted, Sandy nodded. 'I promise.'

What crazy impulse had made her come out with that? Wanting to please Ben?

Or maybe it was the thought of what she would have liked to happen if it was her grandmother, injured, in pain, and having to beg a stranger to help her.

Ida's eyes connected with hers. 'Thank you. Come and see me in the hospital,' she said, before relaxing with a sigh back onto the gurney.

'Right. That's settled.' Ben slapped the side of the ambulance, turned to the ambulance officer. 'I'll ride in the back with my aunt.'

A frail but imperious hand rose. 'You show your friend around Bay Books. Settle her in.'

Sandy had to fight a smile as she watched Ben do battle with his great-aunt to let him accompany her to the hospital.

Minutes later she stood by Ben's side, watching

the tail-lights of the ambulance disappear into the rain. Kate was in the back with Ida.

'Your aunt Ida is quite a lady,' Sandy said, biting her lip to suppress her grin.

'You bet,' said Ben, with a wry smile of his own.

'Isn't she the aunt who…?' She held up her hand. 'Wait. Let me remember. I know!' she said triumphantly. 'The aunt who ran off with an around-the-world sailor?'

Ben's eyes widened. 'You remember that? From all that time ago?'

I remember because you—and the family I fantasised about marrying into—were so important to me. The words were on the tip of her tongue, but she didn't—couldn't—put her voice to them. 'Of course,' she said instead. 'Juicy scandals tend to stick in my mind.'

'It *was* a scandal. For these parts anyway. She was the town spinster, thirty-five and unmarried.'

'Spinster? Ouch! What an awful word.' She giggled. 'Hey, I'm thirty and unmarried. Does that make me—' she made quotation marks in the air with her fingers '—a spinster?'

'As if,' Ben said with a grin. 'Try *career woman about town*—isn't that more up to date?'

'Sounds better. But the message is the same.' She pulled a mock glum face.

Ben stilled, and suddenly he wasn't joking. He looked into her face for a long, intense minute. An emotion she didn't recognise flashed through his eyes and then was gone.

'That boyfriend of yours was an idiot,' he said gruffly.

He lifted a hand as if he was about to touch her, maybe run his finger down her cheek to her mouth like he'd used to.

She tensed, waiting, not sure if she wanted him to or not. Awareness hung between them like the shimmer off the sea on a thirty-eight-degree day.

He moved a step closer. So close she could clearly see that sexy scar on his mouth. She wondered how it would feel if he kissed her...if he took her in his arms...

Her heart began to hammer in her chest so violently surely he must hear it. Her mouth went suddenly dry.

But then, abruptly, he dropped his hand back by his side, stepped away. 'He didn't deserve you,' he said, in a huskier-than-ever voice.

She breathed out, not realising she had been holding her breath. Not knowing whether to feel disappointed or relieved that there was now a safe, non-kissing zone between her and the man she'd once loved.

She cleared her throat, disconcerted by the certain knowledge that if Ben had kissed her she wouldn't have pushed him away. No. She would have swayed closer and...

She took a steadying breath. 'Yeah. Well... I...I'm

better off without him. And soon I'll be living so far away it won't matter one little bit that he chose his mega-wealthy boss's daughter over me.'

She wouldn't take cheating Jason back in a million years. But sometimes it was difficult to keep up the bravado, mask the pain of the way he'd treated her. It was a particular kind of heartbreak to be presented with a *fait accompli* and no opportunity to make things right. It made it very difficult for her to risk her heart again.

'Still hurts, huh?' Ben said, obviously not fooled by her words.

She remembered how he'd used to tease her about her feelings always showing on her face.

She shook her head. After a lacklustre love life she'd thought she'd got things right with Jason. But she wasn't going to admit to Ben that Jason had proved to be another disappointment.

'You talk the talk, Sandy,' Jason had said. *'But you always held back, were never really there for me.'*

She couldn't see the truth in that—would never have committed to living with Jason if she hadn't believed she loved him. If she hadn't believed he would change his mind about marriage.

'Only my pride was hurt,' she said now to Ben. 'Things between us weren't right for a long time. I wasn't happy, and he obviously wasn't either. It had to end somehow....' She took a deep breath. 'And here I am, making a fresh start.' She nodded decisively. 'Now, that's enough about me. Tell me more about your aunt Ida.'

'Sure,' he said, glad for the change in subject. 'Ida got married to her wayfaring sailor on some exotic island somewhere and sailed around the world with him on his yacht until he died. Then she came back here and started the bookshop—first at the other end of town and now in the row of new shops I built.'

'So you're her landlord?'

'The other guy was ripping her off on her rent.'

And Ben always looked after his own.

Sandy remembered how fiercely protective he'd been of his family. How stubbornly loyal. He would have been just as protective of his wife and son.

No wonder he had gone away when he'd lost them. What had brought him back to Dolphin Bay, with its tragic memories?

He turned to face her, his face composed, no hint from his expression that he might have been about to kiss her just minutes ago.

'It was good of you to play along with me to make her happy. I just had to get her into that ambulance and on her way. Thank you.'

She shrugged. 'No problem. I'd like someone to do the same for my grandmother.'

He glanced down at his watch. 'Now you'd better go have your lunch before they close down the kitchen. Sorry I can't join you, but—'

'But what?' Sandy tilted her head to one side. She put up her hand in a halt sign. 'Am I missing something here? Aren't you meant to be showing me the bookshop?'

Ben swivelled back to face her. He frowned. 'Why would you want to see the bookshop?'

'Because I've volunteered to look after it for your aunt until you find someone else. I promised. Remember? Crossed my heart and—'

He cut across her words. 'But that wasn't serious. That was just you playing along with me so she'd go to the hospital. Just a tactic…'

Vehemently, she shook her head. 'A tactic? No it wasn't. I meant it, Ben. I said I'd help out for a few days and I keep my word.'

'But don't you have an interview in Melbourne?'

'Not until next Friday, and today's only Saturday. I was planning on meandering slowly down the coast…'

She thought regretfully of the health spa she'd hoped to check in to for a few days of much needed pampering. Then she thought of the concern in Ida's eyes.

'But it's okay. I'm happy to play bookshop for a while. Really.'

'There's no need to stay, Sandy. It won't be a problem to close the shop for a few days until I find a temporary manager.'

'That's not what your aunt thinks,' she said. 'Besides, it might be useful for my interview to say I've been managing a shop.' She did the quote thing again with her fingers. '"Recent retail experience"—

yes, that would look good on my résumé.' An update on her university holiday jobs working in department stores.

Ben was so tight-lipped he was bordering on grim. 'Sandy, it's nice of you, but forget it. I'll find someone. There are agencies for emergency staff.'

Why was he so reluctant to accept such an easy solution to his aunt's dilemma? Especially when he'd been the one to suggest it?

It wasn't fair to blame her for not being aware of his 'tactic'. And she wasn't—repeat *wasn't*—going to let his lack of enthusiasm at the prospect of her working in the bookshop daunt her.

Slowly, she shook her head from side to side. 'Ben, I gave my word to your great-aunt and I intend to keep it.'

She looked to the doorway of Bay Books. Forced her voice to sound steady. 'C'mon, show me around. I'm dying to see inside.'

Ben hesitated. He took a step forward and then stopped. His face reminded her of those storm clouds that had banked up on the horizon.

Sandy sighed out loud. She made her voice mock scolding. 'Ben, I wouldn't like to be in your shoes if you have to tell your aunt I skipped out on her.'

His jaw clenched. He looked at her without speaking for a long second. 'Is that blackmail, Sandy?'

She couldn't help a smile. 'Not really. But, like I said, if I make a promise I keep it.'

'Do you?' he asked hoarsely.

The smile froze on her face.

Ben stood, his hands clenched by his sides. Was he remembering those passionately sworn promises to keep their love alive even though she was going back to Sydney at the end of her holiday?

Promises she hadn't kept because she'd never heard from him? And she'd been too young, too scared, to take the initiative herself.

She'd been wrong not to persist in trying to keep in touch with him. Wrong not to have trusted him. Now she could see that. Twelve years too late she could see that.

'Yes,' she said abruptly and—unable to face him—turned on her heel. 'C'mon, I need to check out the displays and you need to show me how to work the register and what to do about special orders and all that kind of stuff.'

She knew she was chattering too quickly, but she had to cover the sudden awkwardness between them.

She braced herself and looked back over her shoulder. Was he just going to stay standing on the footpath, looking so forbidding?

No. With an exhaled sigh that she hoped was more exasperated than angry, he followed her through the door of Bay Books.

As Ben walked behind Sandy—forcing himself not to be distracted by the sway of her shapely behind—he cursed himself for being such an idiot. His impulsive ploy to placate Idy with a white lie about Sandy staying to help out had backfired badly.

How could he have forgotten just what a thoughtful, generous person Sandy could be? In that way she hadn't changed since she was eighteen, insisting on helping his mother wash the dishes at the guesthouse even though she'd been a paying guest.

Of course Sandy wouldn't lie to his great-aunt. He should have realised that. And now here she was, insisting on honouring her 'promise'.

The trouble was, the last thing he wanted was his old girlfriend in town, reminding him of what he'd once felt for her. What he didn't want to feel again. Not for her. Not for anyone.

Point-blank, he did *not* want Sandy helping out at Bay Books. Did not want to be faced by her positive get-up-and-go-for-it attitude, her infectious laugh and—he couldn't deny it—her lovely face and sexier-than-ever body.

He gritted his teeth and determined not to fall victim to her charm.

But as she moved through the store he couldn't help but be moved by her unfeigned delight in what some people called his great-aunt's latest folly.

He saw the familiar surrounds afresh through her eyes—the wooden bookcases with their frolicking dolphin borders, the magnificent carved wooden counter, the round tables covered in heavy fringed cloths and stacked with books both bestsellers and more off-beat choices, the lamps thoughtfully positioned, the exotic carpets, the promotional posters artfully displayed, the popular children's corner.

'I love it—I just love it,' she breathed. 'This is how a bookshop should be. Small. Intimate. Connected to its customers.'

Reverently, she stroked the smooth wooden surface of the countertop, caressed with slender pink-tipped fingers the intricate carved dolphins that supported each corner.

'I've never seen anything like it.'

'It's different, all right. On her travels Aunt Ida became good friends with a family of Balinese woodcarvers. She commissioned them to fit out the shop. Had all this shipped over.'

Sandy looked around her, her eyes huge with wonder. 'It's unique. Awesome. No wonder your aunt wants it in safe hands.'

Some people might find the shop too quaint. Old-fashioned in a world of minimalist steel and glass. Redundant at a time of electronic everything. But obviously not Sandy. He might have expected she'd appreciate Aunt Ida's eccentric creation. Just as she'd loved his family's old guesthouse.

She twirled around in the space between the counter and a crammed display of travel paperbacks.

'It even smells wonderful in here. The wood, of course. And that special smell of books. I don't know what it is—the paper, the binding.' She closed her eyes and inhaled with a look of ecstasy. 'I could just breathe it in all day.'

No.

His fists clenched tight by his sides. That was not what he wanted to hear. He didn't want Sandy to fit back in here to Dolphin Bay as if she'd never left.

He wanted her gone, back on that highway and heading south. Not connecting so intuitively with the magic his great-aunt had tried to create here. Not being part of his life just by her very presence.

How could he bear to have her practically next door? Every day she'd be calling on him to ask advice on how to run the shop. Seeking his help. Needing him.

And he wouldn't be able to resist helping her. Might even find himself looking in on the off chance that she needed some assistance with Aunt Ida's oddball accounting methods. Maybe bringing her a coffee from the hotel café. Suggesting they chat about the business over lunch.

That couldn't happen. He wouldn't let it happen. He needed his life to stay just the way it was. He didn't want to invite love into his life again. And with Sandy there would be no second measures.

Sandy threw herself down on the low, overstuffed sofa his aunt provided for customers to sit on and browse through the books, then jumped up again almost straight away. She clasped her hands together, her eyes shining with enthusiasm. 'It's perfect. I am *so* going to enjoy myself here.'

'It's only for a few days,' he warned. 'I'll talk

to the agency straight away.' Again his voice was harsher than he'd intended, edged with fear.

She frowned and he winced at the quick flash of hurt in her eyes. She paused. Her voice was several degrees cooler when she replied.

'I know that, Ben. I'm just helping out until you get a manager. And I'm glad I can, now that I see how much of her heart your aunt has put into her shop.'

Avoiding his eyes, she stepped behind the counter, placed her hands on the countertop and looked around her. Despite his lack of encouragement, there was an eagerness, an excitement about her that he found disconcerting. And way too appealing.

She pressed her lips firmly together. 'I'll try not to bother you too much,' she said. 'But I'll need your help with operating the register. Oh, and the computer, too. Is all her inventory in special files?'

He knew he should show some gratitude for her helping out. After all, he'd been the one to make the ill-conceived suggestion that she should stay. But he was finding it difficult when he knew how dangerous it might be to have Sandy around. Until now he'd been keeping everything together in his under-control life. Or so he'd thought.

'I can show you the register,' he said grudgingly. 'The computer—that's a mystery. But you won't be needing to operate that. And, besides, it's only temporary, right?'

'Yeah. *Very* temporary—as you keep reminding me.'

This time she met his gaze head-on.

'But what makes you think I won't want to do as good a job as I can for your aunt Ida while I'm here? You heard what she said about needing every day of business.'

'I would look after her if she got into trouble.'

The truth was he didn't need the rent his great-aunt insisted on paying him. Could easily settle her overheads.

'Maybe she doesn't want to be looked after? Maybe she wants to be totally independent. I hope I'll be the same when I'm her age.'

Sandy at seventy-five years old? A quick image came to him of her with white hair, all skewered up in a bun on top of her head, and every bit as feisty as his great-aunt.

'I'm sure you will be,' he said, and he forced himself not to smile at the oddly endearing thought. Or, by way of comparison, look too appreciatively at the beautiful woman who was Sandy now, on her thirtieth birthday.

'What about paying the bills?' she asked.

'I'll take care of that.'

'In other words,' she said with a wry twist to her mouth, 'don't forget that I'm just a temporary caretaker?'

'Something like that,' he agreed, determined not to make it easy for her. Though somewhere, hidden deep behind the armour he wore around his feelings, he wished he didn't have to act so tough. But if he didn't protect himself he might fall apart—and he couldn't risk that.

She looked up at him, her expression both teasing and serious at the same time. But her voice wasn't as confident as it had been. There was a slight betraying quiver that wrenched at him.

'You know something, Ben? I'm beginning to think you don't want me in Dolphin Bay,' she said, her eyes huge, her luscious mouth trembling. She took a deep breath. 'Am I right?'

He stared at her, totally unable to say anything.

Images flashed through his mind like frames from a flickering cinema screen.

Sandy at that long-ago surf club dance, her long hair flying around her, laughing as she and her sister tried to mimic Kate's outrageously sexy dancing, smiling shyly when she noticed him watching her.

Sandy breathless and trembling in his arms as he kissed her for the first time.

Sandy in the tiniest of bikinis, overcoming her fear to bravely paddle out on her body-board to meet him where the big waves were breaking.

Sandy, her eyes red and her face blotchy and tear-stained, running to him again and again to hurl herself in his arms for just one more farewell kiss as her father impatiently honked the horn on the family car taking her back to Sydney.

Then nothing. *Nothing.*

Until now.

He fisted his hands so tightly it hurt the harsh edges of the scars. Scars that were constant reminders of the agony of his loss.

How in hell could he answer her question?

CHAPTER FOUR

HE SAID *SHE* showed her emotions on her face? She didn't need a PhD in psychology to read his, either. It was only too apparent he was just buying time before spilling the words he knew she wouldn't want to hear.

For an interminable moment he said nothing. Shifted his weight from foot to foot. Then he uttered just one drawn-out word. 'Well…'

He didn't need to say anything else.

Sandy swallowed hard against the sudden, unexpected shaft of hurt. Forced her voice to sound casual, light-hearted. 'Hey, I was joking, but…but you're serious. You really *don't* want me around, do you?'

She pushed the rain-damp hair away from her face with fingers that weren't quite steady. Gripped the edge of the countertop hard, willing the trembling to stop.

When he finally spoke his face was impassive, his voice schooled, his eyes shuttered. 'You're right. I don't think it's a great idea.'

She couldn't have felt worse if he'd slapped her. She fought the flush of humiliation that burned her cheeks. Forced herself to meet his gaze without flinching. 'Why? Because we dated when we were kids?'

'As soon as people make the connection that you're my old girlfriend there'll be gossip, speculation. I don't want that.'

She swallowed hard against a suddenly dry throat, forced the words out. 'Because of your…because of Jodi?'

'That too.'

The counter was a barrier between them but he was close. Touching distance close. So close she could smell the salty, clean scent of him—suddenly heart-achingly familiar. After their youthful making out sessions all those years ago she had relished the smell of him on her, his skin on her skin, his mouth on her mouth. Hadn't wanted ever to shower it away.

'But…mainly because of me.'

His words were so quiet she had to strain to hear them over the noise of the rain on the metal roof above.

Bewildered, she shook her head. 'Because of you? I don't get it.'

'Because things are different, Sandy. It isn't only the town that's changed.'

His voice was even. Too even. She sensed it was a struggle for him to keep it under control.

He turned his broad shoulders so he looked past

her and through the shop window, into the distance towards the bay as he spoke. 'Did Kate tell you everything about the fire that killed Jodi and my son, Liam?'

'No.' Sandy shook her head, suddenly dreading what she might hear. Not sure she could cope with it. Her knees felt suddenly shaky, and she leaned against the countertop for support.

Ben turned back to her and she gasped at the anguish he made no effort to mask.

'He was only a baby, Sandy, not even a year old. I couldn't save them. I was in the volunteer fire service and I was off fighting a blaze somewhere else. Everything was tinder-dry from years of drought. We thought Dolphin Bay was safe, but the wind turned. Those big gum trees near the guesthouse caught alight. And then the building. The guests got out. But…but not…' His head dropped as his words faltered.

He'd said before that he didn't want to talk about his tragedy—now it was obvious he couldn't find any more words. With a sudden aching realisation she knew it would never get easier for him.

'Don't,' she murmured, feeling beyond terrible that she'd forced him to relive those unbearable moments. She put her hand up to halt him, maybe to touch him, then let it drop again. 'You don't have to tell me any more.'

Big raindrops sat on his eyelashes like tears. She

ached to wipe them away. To do something, anything, to comfort him.

But he'd just said he didn't want her here in town.

He raised his head to face her again. 'I lost everything that day,' he said, his eyes bleak. 'I have nothing to give you.'

She swallowed hard, glanced again at the scars on his hands, imagined him desperately trying to reach his wife and child in the burning guesthouse before it was too late. She realised there were scars where she couldn't see them. Worse scars than the visible ones.

'I'm not asking anything of you, Ben. Just maybe to be…to be friends.'

She couldn't stop her voice from breaking—was glad the rain meant they had the bookshop all to themselves. That no one could overhear their conversation.

He turned his tortured gaze full on to her and she flinched before it.

The words were torn from him. 'Friends? Can you really be "just friends" with someone you once loved?'

She picked up a shiny hardback from the pile to the left of her on the counter, put it back without registering the title. Then she turned back to face him. Took a deep breath. 'Was it really love? We were just kids.'

'It was for me,' he said, his voice gruff and very serious, his hands clenched tightly by his sides. 'It hurt that you never answered my letters, never got in touch.'

'It hurt me that you never wrote like you said you would,' she breathed, remembering as if it were yesterday the anguish of his rejection. Oh, yes, it had been love for her too.

But a small voice deep inside whispered that perhaps she had got over him faster than he had got over her. She'd never forgotten him but she'd moved on, and the memories of her first serious crush had become fainter and fainter. Sometimes it had seemed as though Ben and the times she'd had with him at Dolphin Bay had been a kind of dream.

She hadn't fully appreciated then what was apparent now—Ben wasn't a player, like Jason or her father. When he loved, he loved for keeps. In the intervening years she'd been attracted to men who reminded her of him and been bitterly disappointed when they fell short. She could see now there was only one man like Ben.

They both spoke at the same time.

'Why—?'

'Why—?'

Then answered at the same time.

'My father—'

'Your father—'

Sandy gave a short nervous laugh. 'And my mother, too,' she added, turning away from him, looking down at a display of mini-books of inspirational thoughts, shuffling them backwards and forwards. 'She told me not to chase after you when you were so obviously not interested. Even my sister, Lizzie, got fed up with me crying over you and told me to get over it and move on.'

'My dad said the same thing about you. That you had your own life in the city. That you wouldn't give me a thought when you were back in the bright lights. That we were too young, anyway.' He snorted. '*Too young.* He and my mother got married when they were only a year older than I was then.'

She looked up to face him. 'I phoned the guesthouse, you know, but your father answered. I was too chicken to speak to him, though I suspect he knew it was me. He told me not to call again.'

'He never said.'

Sandy could hear the beating of her own heart over the sound of the rain on the roof. 'We were young. Maybe too young to doubt them—or defy them.'

An awkward silence—a silence choked by the echoes of words unspoken, of kisses unfulfilled— fell between them until finally she knew she had to be the one to break it.

'I wonder what would have happened if we had—'

'Don't go there, Sandy,' he said.

She took a step back from his sudden vehemence, banging her hip on the wooden fin of a carved dolphin. But she scarcely felt the pain.

'Never torture yourself with *what if?* and *if only,*'

he continued. 'Remember what you said? Water under the bridge.'

'It…it was a long time ago.'

She didn't know what else she could say. Couldn't face thinking of the 'what ifs?' Ben must have struggled with after the fire.

While he was recalling anguish and irredeemable loss, she was desperately fighting off the memories of how much fun they'd had together all those years ago.

She'd been so serious, so strait-laced, so under her father's thumb. For heaven's sake, she'd been old enough to vote but had never stayed out after midnight. Ben had helped her lighten up, take risks—be reckless, even. All the time knowing he'd be there for her if she stumbled.

He hadn't been a bad boy by any means, but he'd been an exciting boy—an irreverent boy who'd thumbed his nose at her father's old-fashioned edicts and made her question the ways she'd taken for granted. So many times she'd snuck out to meet him after dark, her heart thundering with both fear of what would happen if she were caught and anticipation of being alone with him.

How good it had felt when he'd kissed her—kissed her at any opportunity when they could be by themselves. How his kisses, his caresses, had stirred her body, awakening yearnings she hadn't known she was capable of.

Yearnings she'd never felt as strongly since. Not even for Jason.

Saying no to going all the way with Ben that summer was one of the real regrets of her life. Losing her virginity to him would have been an unforgettable experience. How could it not have been when their passion had been so strong?

She couldn't help remembering their last kiss—with her father about to drag her into the car—fired by unfulfilled passion and made more poignant in retrospect because she'd had no idea that it would be her last kiss from Ben.

Did he remember it too?

She searched his face, but he seemed immersed in his own dark thoughts.

Wearily, she wiped her hand over her forehead as if she could conjure up answers. Why had those kisses been printed so indelibly on her memory? Unleashed passion? Hormones? Pheromones? Was it the magic of first love? Or was it a unique power that came only from Ben?

Ben who had grown into this intense, unreadable, tormented man whom she could not even pretend to know any more.

The rain continued to fall. It muffled the sound of the cars swishing by outside the bookshop, made it seem as if they were in their own world, cocooned by their memories from the reality of everyday life in Dolphin Bay. From all that had happened in the twelve years since they'd last met.

Ben cleared his throat, leaned a little closer to her over the barrier of the counter.

'I'm glad you told me you never got my letters, that you tried to phone,' he said, his voice gruff. 'I never understood how you could just walk away from what we had.'

'Me too. I never understood how you didn't want to see me again, I mean.'

She thought of the tears she'd wept into her pillow all those years ago. How abandoned she'd felt. How achingly lonely. Even the agony of Jason's betrayal hadn't come near it.

Then she forced her thoughts to return to today. To Ben's insistence that he didn't want her hanging around Dolphin Bay, even to help his injured aunt at a time of real need for the old lady.

It was beyond hurtful.

Consciously, she straightened her shoulders. She forced a brave, unconcerned edge to her voice. 'But now we know the wrong my father did maybe we can forget old hurts and…and feel some kind of closure.'

'Closure?' Ben stared at her. 'What kind of psychobabble is *that*?'

Psychobabble? She felt rebuffed by his response. She'd actually thought 'closure' was a very well-chosen word. Under the circumstances.

'What I mean is…maybe we can try to be friends? Forgive the past. Forget there was anything else between us?'

She was lying. *Oh, how she was lying.*

While her mind dictated emotion-free words like 'closure' and 'friends' her body was shouting out that she found him every bit as desirable as she had twelve years ago. More so.

Just months ago—when she'd still had a job—she'd worked on a campaign for a hot teen surf clothing label. Ben at nineteen would have been perfectly cast in the lead male role, surrounded by adoring bikini-clad girls.

Now, Ben at thirty-one could star as a hunky action man in any number of very grown-up commercials. His face was only improved by his cropped hair, the deep tan, the slight crinkles around his eyes and that intriguing scar on his mouth. His damp shirt moulded to a muscled chest and powerful shoulders and arms.

Now they were both adults. Experienced adults. She'd been the world's most inexperienced eighteen-year-old. What would she feel if she kissed him now? A shudder ran deep inside her. There would be no stopping at kisses, that was for sure.

'You may be able to forget we were more than friends but I can't,' he said hoarsely. 'I still find you very attractive.'

So he felt it too.

Something so powerful that twelve years had done nothing to erode it.

Her heart did that flippy thing again, over and over, stealing her breath, her composure. Before she could stutter out something in response he continued.

'That's why I don't want you in Dolphin Bay.'

She gasped at his bluntness.

'I don't mean to sound rude,' he said. 'I…I just can't deal with having you around.'

What could she say in response? For all her skill as an award-winning copywriter, she couldn't find the right words in the face of such raw anguish. All she could do was nod.

That vein throbbed at his temple. 'I don't want to be reminded of what it was like to…to have feelings for someone when I can't…don't want to ever feel like that again.'

The pain behind his confession made her catch her breath in another gasp. It overwhelmed the brief flash of pleasure she'd felt that he still found her attractive. And it hurt that he was so pointedly rejecting her.

'Right,' she said.

Such an inadequate word. Woefully inadequate.

'Right,' she repeated. She cleared her throat. Looked anywhere but at him. 'I hear what you're saying. Loud and clear.'

'I'm sorry, I—'

She put up her hand in a halt sign. 'Don't be. I…I appreciate your honesty.'

Her heart went out to him. Not in pity but in empathy. She had known pain. Not the kind of agony he'd endured, but pain just the same. Her parents' divorce. Jason's callous dumping. Betrayal by the friends who'd chosen to be on Jason's side in the break-up and had accepted invitations to today's wedding of the year at St Mark's, Darling Point, the Sydney church famed for society weddings.

But the philosophy she'd evolved in those years when she'd been fighting her father's blockade on letting her lead a normal teenage life had been to refuse to let hurt and disappointment hold her back for long. She now firmly believed that good things were always around the corner. That light always followed darkness. But you had to take steps to invite that light into your life. As she had in planning to leave all the reminders of her life with Jason behind her.

Ben had suffered a tragedy she could not even begin to imagine. Would he ever be able to move out of the shadows?

'Honesty is best all round,' he said, the jagged edge to his voice giving a terrible sincerity to the cliché.

She gritted her teeth against the thought of all Ben had endured since they'd last met, the damage it had done to him. And yet…

From what she remembered of sweet-faced Jodi Hart, she couldn't imagine she would want to see the husband she'd loved wrapping himself in a shroud of grief and self-blame, not allowing himself ever again to feel happiness or love.

But it was not for her to make that judgement.

She, too, belonged to Ben's yesterday, and that was where he seemed determined to keep her. He did not want to be part of her tomorrow in any way.

If only she could stop wondering if the magic would still be there for them…if they could both overcome past hurts enough to try.

She had to force herself not to sigh out loud. The attraction she felt for him was still there, would never go away. It was a longing so powerful it hurt.

'Now I know where I stand,' she said, summoning the strength to make her voice sound normal.

He was right. It was best to get it up-front. Ben was not for her. Not any more. The barriers he had up against her were so entrenched they were almost visible.

But in spite of it all she refused to regret her impulsive decision to return to Dolphin Bay. It was healing to meet up with Ben and discover that he hadn't, after all, heartlessly ditched her all those years ago. Coming after the Jason fiasco, that revelation was a great boost to her self-esteem.

She forced a smile. 'That's sorted, then. Let's get back on track. Tell me more about Bay Books. I'm going to be the best darn temporary manager you'll ever see.'

'So long as you know it's just that. Temporary.'

She nodded. She could do this. After all, she loved reading and she loved books—e-books, audiobooks, but especially the real thing. Added to that, the experience of looking after the bookshop might help her snag the candle store franchise. Maybe her reckless promise to Ida might turn out to benefit herself as much as Ben's great-aunt.

Yes, making that swift exit off the highway this morning had definitely been a good idea. But in five days she would get back into her green Beetle and put Dolphin Bay and Ben Morgan behind her again.

Five days of wanting Ben but knowing it could never be.

Five days to eradicate the yearning, once and for all.

But the cup-half-full part of her bobbed irrepressibly to the surface. There was one other way to look at it: five days to convince him they should be friends again. And after that who knew?

CHAPTER FIVE

BEN WATCHED THE emotions as they played across Sandy's face. Finally her expression settled at something between optimistic and cheerful.

He might have been fooled if he hadn't noticed the tight grip of her hands on the edge of the countertop. Even after all these years and a high-powered job in advertising she hadn't learned to mask her feelings.

He had hurt her. Hurt her with his blunt statements. Hurt her with his rejection of her friendship, his harsh determination to protect himself from her and the feelings she evoked.

He hated to cause her pain. He would fight with his fists anyone who dared to injure her in any way. But he had to be up-front. She had to know the score. The fire had changed him, snatched his life from him, forged a different person from the one Sandy remembered. *He had nothing left to give her.*

Her eyes were guarded, the shadows beneath them more deeply etched. She tilted her head to one side. A wispy lock of rain-damp hair fell across her face. He had to force himself not to reach out and tenderly push it aside, as he would have done twelve years ago.

She took a deep breath and again he couldn't help but appreciate the enticing swell of her breasts. She'd been sizzling at eighteen. As a woman of thirty she was sexual dynamite. Ignite it and he was done for.

Finally she spoke. 'Okay, so maybe promising to help your aunt wasn't such a great idea. But I crossed my heart. I'm here in Dolphin Bay. Whether you like it or not.'

Her lovely pink-stained mouth trembled and she bit down firmly on her lower lip. She blinked rapidly, as if fighting back tears, sending a wrenching shaft of pain straight to his heart.

She choked out her words. 'Don't be angry at me for insisting on staying. I couldn't bear that.'

'Like I'd do *that*, Sandy. Surely you know me better?'

She shook her head slowly from side to side. Her voice broke like static. 'Ben, I don't know you at all any more.'

A bruised silence fell between them. He was powerless to do anything to end it. Each breath felt like an effort.

Sandy's shoulders were hunched somewhere around her ears. He watched her make an effort to pull them down.

'If you don't want to be friends, where does that put us?'

'Seems to me we're old friends who've moved on

but who have been thrown together by circumstance. Can't we leave it at that?'

Before she had a chance to mask it, disappointment clouded her eyes. She looked away. It was a long moment before she nodded and looked back up at him. Her voice was resolute, as if she were closing on a business deal, with only the slightest tremor to betray her. 'You're right. Of course you're right. We'll be grown-up about this. Passing polite for the next five days. Is that the deal?'

She offered him her hand to shake.

He looked at it for a long moment, at her narrow wrist and slender fingers. Touching Sandy wasn't a good idea. Not after all these years. Not when he remembered too well how good she'd felt in his arms. How much he wanted her—had always wanted her.

He hesitated a moment too long and she dropped her hand back by her side.

He'd hurt her again. He gritted his teeth. What kind of a man was he that he couldn't shake her hand?

'That's settled, then,' she said, her voice brisk and businesslike, her eyes not meeting his. 'By the way, I'll need somewhere to sleep. Any suggestions?'

Wham! What kind of sucker punch was that? His reaction was instant—raw, physical hunger for her. Hunger so powerful it knocked him for six.

He knew what he ached to say. *You can sleep in my bed. With me. Naked, with your legs twined around mine. On top of me. Beneath me. With your face flushed with desire and your heart racing with passion. Sleep with me so we can finish what we started so long ago.*

Instead he clenched his fists by his sides, looked somewhere over her head so he wouldn't have to see her face. He couldn't let her guess the thoughts that were taking over his mind and body.

'You'll be my guest at the hotel. I'll organise a room for you as soon as I get back.'

She put up her hand. 'But that won't be necessary. I—'

He cut short her protest. 'No buts. You're helping my family. You don't pay for accommodation. You'll go in a penthouse suite.'

She shook her head. 'I'm happy to pay, but if you insist—'

'I insist.' He realised, with some relief, that the rain had stopped pelting on the roof. 'The weather has let up. We'll get you checked in now.'

The twist to her mouth conceded defeat, although he suspected the argument was far from over. Like Idy, she was fiercely independent. Back then she'd always insisted on paying her way on their dates. Even if she only matched him ice cream for ice cream or soft drink for soft drink.

'Okay. Thanks. I'll just grab my handbag and—' She felt around on the counter, looked around her in panic. 'My bag!'

'It's at Reception. Kate picked it up.'

Kate, her eyes wide with interest and speculation,

had whispered to him as they were helping Ida into the ambulance. She said Sandy had been in such a hurry to follow him out of the restaurant and onto the sand she'd left her bag behind.

Kate obviously saw that as significant. He wondered how many people now knew his old girlfriend was back in town.

The phone calls would start soon. His mother first up. She'd liked Sandy. She'd never pried into his and his brother Jesse's teenage love lives. But she'd be itching to know why Sandy was back in town.

And he'd wager that Sandy would have a stream of customers visiting Bay Books. Customers whose interest was anything but literary.

Sandy went to move from behind the counter.

'Sandy, before you go, there's something I've been meaning to tell you.'

She frowned. 'Yes?'

He'd been unforgivably ill-mannered not to shake her hand just to avoid physical contact. So what inexplicable force made him now lean towards her and lightly brush his thumb over her mouth where it was stained that impossibly bright pink? He could easily tell her what he had to without touching her.

His pulse accelerated a gear at the soft, yielding feel of her lips, the warm female scent of her. She quivered in awareness of his touch, then stood very still, her cheeks flushed and her eyes wide.

He didn't want her around. Didn't want her warmth, her laughter, falling on his heart like drops of water on a spiky-leaved plant so parched it was in danger of dying. A plant that needed the sun, the life-giving rain, but felt safe and comfortable existing in the shadows, living a half-life that until now had seemed enough.

'Sandy....' There was so much more he wanted to say. But couldn't.

She looked mutely back at him.

He drew a deep, ragged breath. Cleared his throat. Forced his voice into its usual tone, aware that it came out gruffer but unable to do anything about it.

'I don't know if this is the latest city girl look, but your mouth…it's kinda pink in the middle. You might want to fix it.'

She froze, then her hand shot to her mouth. 'What do you mean? I don't use pink lipstick.'

Without saying a word he walked around to her side of the counter and pulled out a drawer. He handed her the mirror his aunt always kept there.

Sandy looked at her image. She stared. She shrieked. 'That's the ink from my niece Amy's feather pen!'

It was difficult not to grin at her reaction.

Then she glared at him, her eyes sparking, though she looked about as ferocious as one of the stray puppies his mother fostered. '*You!* You let me go around all this time looking like this? Why didn't you tell me?'

He shrugged, finding it hard not show his amusement at her outraged expression. 'How was I to know it wasn't some fashion thing? I've seen girls wearing black nail polish that looks like bruises.'

'But this…' She wiped her hand ineffectively across her mouth. 'This! I look like a circus clown.'

He shrugged. 'I think it's kinda cute. In a…circusy kind of way.'

'You!' She scrutinised her image and scrubbed hard at her mouth.

Now her lips looked all pouty and swollen, like they'd used to after their marathon teen making out sessions. He had to look away. To force himself not to remember.

She glared again. 'Don't you ever, *ever* let me go out in public again looking weird, okay?'

'I said cute, not weird. But okay.' He couldn't help his mouth from lifting into a grin.

Her eyes narrowed into accusing slits. 'Are you laughing at me, Ben Morgan?'

'Never,' he said, totally negating his words by laughing.

She tried, but she couldn't sustain the glare. Her mouth quirked into a grin that spilled into laughter chiming alongside his.

After all the angst of the morning it felt good to laugh. Again he felt something shifting and stirring deep inside the seized and rusted engine of his emotions. He didn't want it to fire into life again. That way led to pain and anguish. But already Sandy's laughter, her scent, her unexpected presence again in his life, was like the slow drip-drip-drip of some powerful repair oil.

'C'mon,' he said. 'While the rain's stopped let's get you checked into the hotel. Then I have to get back to work.'

As he pulled the door of Bay Books closed behind him he found himself pursing his mouth to whistle. A few broken bars of sound escaped before he clamped down on them. He glanced to see if Sandy had noticed, but her eyes were focused on the street ahead.

He hadn't whistled for years.

CHAPTER SIX

SANDY SAT IN her guest room at Hotel Hideous, planning a new list. She shivered and hugged her arms to herself. The room was air conditioned to the hilt. There was no stinting on luxury in the modern, tasteful furnishings. She loved the dolphin motif that was woven into the bedcover and decorative pillows, and repeated discreetly on the borders of the curtains. And the view across the old harbour and the bay was beyond magnificent.

But it wasn't a patch on the charm of the old guest-house. Who could have believed the lovely building would come to such a tragic end? She shuddered at the thought of what Ben had endured. Was she foolish to imagine that he could ever get over his terrible losses? Ever be able to let himself love again?

She forced herself to concentrate as she turned a new page of her fairy notebook. The pretty pink pen had been relegated to the depths of her handbag. She didn't have the heart to throw Amy's gift in the bin, even though she could never use it again.

She still burned at the thought of not just Ben but

Kate, Ida and who-knew-who-else seeing her with the hot pink stain on her mouth. It was hardly the sophisticated image she'd thought she was putting across. Thankfully, several minutes of scrubbing with a toothbrush had eliminated the stain.

But maybe the ink stain had, in a roundabout way, served a purpose. Thoughtfully, she stroked her lip with her finger, where Ben's thumb had been. After all, hadn't the stain induced Ben to break out of his self-imposed cage and actually touch her?

She took a pen stamped with the Hotel Harbour-side logo—which, of course, incorporated a dolphin—from the desk in front of her and started to write—this time in regulation blue ink.

1. *Reschedule birthday celebrations.*

No.

Postpone indefinitely.

Was turning thirty, with her life such a mess, actually cause for celebration anyway? Maybe it was best left unmarked. She could hope for better next year.

2. *Congratulate self for not thinking once about The Wedding.*

She scored through the T and the W to make them lower case. It was her friends who had dramatised the occasion with capital letters. Her so-called friends who'd gone over to the dark side and accepted their invitations.

She could thank Ben's aunt Ida for pushing all thoughts of That-Jerk-Jason and his lucrative trip down the aisle out of her mind.

Or—and she must be honest—was it really Ida who'd distracted her?

She realised she was gnawing the top of the pen.

3. *Quit chewing on pens for once and for all. Especially pens that belong to first love.*

First love now determined not even to be friends. Which brought her to the real issue.

4. *Forget Ben Morgan.*

She stabbed it into the paper.

Forget the shivery delight that had coursed through her when his finger had traced the outline of her mouth. Forget how he'd looked when he had laughed—laughed at her crazy pink ink stain—forget the light in his eyes, the warmth of his smile. Forget the stupid, illogical hope that sprang into her heart when they joked together like in old times.

She slammed the notebook shut, sending glitter shimmering over the desk. Opened it again. She underscored the last words.

Then got on to the next item.

5. *Visit Ida and get info on running bookshop.*

She had to open Bay Books tomorrow and she didn't have a clue what she should be doing. This was scary stuff.

She leaned back in her chair to think about the questions she should ask the older lady when the buzzer to her room sounded.

'Who is it?' she called out, slamming her notebook shut again in a flurry of glitter.

'Ben.'

In spite of her resolutions her heart leaped at the sound of his voice. 'Just give me a second,' she called.

Her hands flew to her face, then smoothed her still-damp-from-the-shower hair. She tightened the belt on the white towelling hotel bathrobe. She ran her tongue around suddenly dry lips before she fumbled with the latch and opened the door.

Ben filled the doorway with his broad shoulders and impressive height. Her heart tripped into double time at the sight of him. He had changed into jeans and a blue striped shirt that brought out the colour of his eyes. Could any man be more handsome?

She stuttered out a greeting, noticed he held a large brown paper grocery bag in one hand.

He thrust the bag at her. 'For you. I'm not good at gift wrapping.'

She looked from the bag up to him. 'Gift wrapping?'

'I feel bad your birthday turned out like this.'

'This is a birthday gift?'

He shrugged. 'A token.'

She flushed, pleased beyond measure at his thoughtfulness. 'I like surprises. Thank you.'

Not sure what to expect, she delved into the bag. It was jam-packed with Snickers bars. 'Ohmigod!' she exclaimed in delighted disbelief.

He shifted from foot to foot. 'You used to like them.'

She smiled at him. 'I still do. They're my favourite.'

She didn't have the heart to add that when she was eighteen she'd been able to devour the chocolate bars by the dozen without gaining weight, but that at thirty they were an occasional indulgence.

'Thank you,' she said. 'You couldn't have given me anything I'd like more.'

She wasn't lying.

Ben's thoughtfully chosen gift in a brown paper bag was way more valuable than any of the impersonal 'must-have' trinkets Jason had used to choose and have gift wrapped by the shop. Her last present from him had been an accessory for her electronic tablet that he had used more than she ever had.

Her heart swelled with affection for Ben. For wounded, difficult, vulnerable Ben.

She looked up at him, aching to throw her arms around him and kiss him. Kiss him for remembering her sweet tooth. Kiss him for the simple honesty of his brown-bagged gift. Kiss him for showing her that, deep down somewhere beneath his scars and defences, her Sir Galahad on a surfboard was still there.

But she felt too wary to do so. She wasn't sure she could handle any more rejection in one day. His words echoed in her head and in her heart: *'I don't want you in Dolphin Bay.'*

'Thank you,' she said again, feeling the words were totally inadequate to express her pleasure at his gesture.

He looked pleased with himself in a very male, tell-me-again-how-clever-I-was way she found endearing.

'I bought all the shop had—which just happened to be thirty.'

She smiled up at him. 'The shopkeeper must have thought you were a greedy pig with a desperate addiction to chocolate.'

'Nah. They know chilli corn chips are more to my taste.'

She hugged the bag of chocolate bars to her chest. 'So I won't have to share? Because you might have to fight me for them.'

'That makes *you* the greedy pig,' he said. 'They're all yours.' He stood still, looking deep into her eyes. 'Happy birthday, Sandy.'

She saw warmth mixed with wariness—which might well be a reflection of what showed in her own eyes.

Silence fell between them. She was aware of her own quickened breathing over the faint hum of the air-conditioning. Felt intoxicated by the salty, so familiar scent of him.

Now.

Surely now was the moment to kiss him? Suddenly she desperately wanted to feel his mouth—that sexy, sexy mouth—on hers. To taste again the memory that had lingered through twelve years away from him.

She felt herself start to sway towards him, her lips parting, her gaze focusing on the blue eyes that seemed to go a deeper shade of blue as he returned her gaze. Her heart was thudding so loudly surely he could hear it.

But as she moved he tensed and took an abrupt step backwards.

She froze. *Rejection again.* When would she learn?

She stepped back too, so hastily she was in danger of tripping backwards into the room. She wrapped her robe tighter around her, focused on the list of hotel safety instructions posted by the door rather than on him. A flush rose up her neck to sting her cheeks.

She couldn't think of a word to say.

After an excruciatingly uncomfortable moment Ben cleared his throat. 'I've been sent on a mission from Aunt Ida to find and retrieve you and take you to the hospital to meet with her.'

Sandy swallowed hard, struggled to make her voice sound light-hearted. 'Sounds serious stuff. Presumably an urgent briefing on the Bay Books project?'

He snapped his fingers. 'Right first guess.'

She smiled, knowing it probably looked forced but determined to appear natural—not as if just seconds ago she'd been longing for his kiss.

'Let me guess again. She's getting anxious about filling me in on how it all works?'

'Correct again,' he said. 'I promised to return with you ASAP to complete the mission.'

'Funnily enough I have no other pressing social engagements in Dolphin Bay.' She turned and started to walk back into the room, then stopped and looked back over her shoulder at him. 'Do you want to come in while I get dressed?'

His glance went briefly to her open neckline. He cleared his throat. 'Not a good idea.'

She blushed even redder and clutched the robe tighter. 'I mean… I didn't mean…' she stuttered.

'How about I come back to get you in half an hour?'

Her voice came out an octave higher. 'Twenty minutes max will be fine. Where will you be if I'm ready earlier?'

'Downstairs in my office.'

'Pick me up in twenty, then.'

He turned to go.

She swallowed against the sudden tension in her throat. 'Ben?' she said.

He swung back to face her, a question on his face.

'Thank you for the Snickers. I won't say I'll treasure them for ever, because they'll be devoured in double quick time. But…thank you.'

'You're welcome,' he said. 'It was—'

Afterwards she wondered at the impulse that had made her forget all caution, all fear of rejection. Before she could think about whether it was a good thing or not to do, propelled by pure instinct, she leaned up on her bare toes and kissed him lightly on his cheek.

Then she staggered at the impact of his closeness, at the memories that came rushing back in a flood of heat and hormones. The feel of his beard-roughened cheek beneath her lips, the strength of his tightly muscled body, the out-and-out maleness of him. She clung to him, overwhelmed by nostalgia for the past, for when she'd had the right to hold him close. *How could she ever have let go of that right?*

His hands grasped her shoulders to steady her. She could feel their warmth on her skin through the thick cloth of her robe. Swiftly, he released her. He muttered something inarticulate.

Reeling, she lifted her head in response, saw the shutters come down over his eyes—but not before she'd glimpsed something she couldn't read. It could have been passion but was more likely panic.

Bad, bad idea, Sandy, she berated herself. *Even a chaste peck is too much for him to handle.*

Too much for you *to handle.*

But no way was she was going to let herself feel ashamed of a friendly thank-you kiss. She was used to spontaneous expressions of affection between friends.

She forced her breath to steady, tilted her chin upwards. 'See you in twenty,' she said, praying he didn't notice the tremor in her voice.

Ben stood back and watched as Sandy talked with his great-aunt in her room at the brand new Dolphin Bay Memorial Hospital. He might have known they would hit it off.

On doctor's orders, Ida was lying flat on her back in her hospital bed. She'd been told she had to hold that position for six weeks to heal her cracked pelvis.

Sandy had pulled up a chair beside her and was chatting away as if she and Ida were old friends.

Why, although they were talking about authors and titles of favourite books, did he sense this instant alliance could mean trouble for him? Trouble not of the business kind—hell, there was nothing he couldn't handle *there*—but a feminine kind of trouble he was not as well equipped to deal with.

Sandy was laughing and gesticulating with her hands as she spoke. His aunt was laughing too. It pleased him to see a warm flush vanquishing the grey tinge of pain from her face.

'What do you think, Ben?' Sandy asked.

'Me?'

'Yes. Who is the primary customer for Bay Books?'

He shrugged. 'People off the boats looking for something to read? Retirees?'

His aunt nodded. 'They're important, yes. But I sell more books to the telecommuters than to anyone else. They're crazy for book clubs. A book club gives them human contact as an antidote to the hours they spend working away on their computers, reporting to an office somewhere miles and miles away.'

Ben rubbed his hands together in simulated glee. 'All those people fleeing the cities, making a seachange to live on the coast—the lifeblood of commerce in Dolphin Bay. They're buying land, building houses, and spending their socks off.'

Sandy wrinkled up her nose in the way he remembered so well. It was just as cute on her at thirty as it had been at eighteen.

'That seems very calculating,' she said.

'What do you expect from the President of the Dolphin Bay Chamber of Commerce?' said Aunt Ida, her voice dripping with the pride all his family felt at his achievement. 'The town has really come on under his leadership.'

Sandy's eyes widened. 'You're full of surprises, Ben.'

On that so expressive face of hers he could see her wondering how he'd come from fisherman's son to successful businessman. Her father had judged him not good enough, not wealthy enough. He'd had no idea of how much land Ben's family owned. And Sandy didn't know how spurred on to succeed Ben had been by the snobby older man's low opinion of him.

'We have a lot to catch up on,' she said.

No.

More than ever he did *not* want to spend more time than was necessary with Sandy, reviving old feelings that were best left buried.

She was modestly dressed now, in a neat-fitting T-shirt and a skirt of some floaty material that covered her knees. But she'd answered the door to him at the hotel wrapped in nothing more than a Hotel Harbourside bathrobe.

As she'd spoken to him the robe had slid open to reveal the tantalising shadow between her breasts. Her face had been flushed and her hair damp. It was obvious she'd just stepped out of the shower and the thought of her naked had been almost more than his libido could take.

Naked in one of his hotel bathrooms. Naked under one of his hotel's bathrobes. It hadn't taken much to take the thought a step further to her naked on one of his hotel's beds. With the hotel's owner taking passionate possession.

He'd had to grit his teeth and force his gaze to somewhere above her head.

When she'd kissed him it had taken every ounce

of his iron-clad self-control not to take her in his arms and kiss her properly. Not on the cheek but claiming her mouth, tasting her with his tongue, exploring her sexy body with hungry hands. Backing her into the room and onto the bed.

No.

There'd be no catching up on old times. Or letting his libido lead him where he had vowed not to go.

He cleared his throat. 'Isn't this conversation irrelevant to you running the bookstore for Aunt Ida?'

Sandy met his gaze in a way that let him know she knew only too well he was steering the conversation away from anything personal.

'Of course. You're absolutely right.'

She turned to face the hospital bed.

'Ida, tell me about any special orders.' Then she looked back at him, her head at a provocative angle. Her eyes gleamed with challenge. 'Is that better, Mr President?'

He looked to Ida for support, but her eyes narrowed as she looked from him to Sandy and back again.

It was starting. The speculation about him and Sandy. The gossip. And it looked as if he couldn't count on his aunt for support in his battle to protect his heart.

In fact she looked mighty pleased at the prospect of uncovering something personal between him and her temporary manager.

'You can tell me more about your past friend-

ship with Sandy some other time, nephew of mine,'
she said.

Sandy looked as uncomfortable as he felt, and had
trouble meeting his gaze. 'Can we get back to talking about Bay Books, Ida?' she asked.

His aunt laughed. 'Back to the not nearly so interesting topic of the bookshop? Okay, my dear, have
you got something you can take some notes in? The
special orders can get complicated.'

Looking relieved, Sandy dived into her handbag.
She pulled out a luminous pink notebook and with it
came a flurry of glitter that sparkled in the shafts of
late-afternoon sun falling on his aunt's hospital bed.

'Sorry about the mess,' she said, biting down on
her bottom lip as the particles settled across the bed-
covers.

Ida seemed mesmerised by the glitter. 'It's not
mess, it's fairy dust!' she exclaimed, clapping her
hands with delight. Her still youthful blue eyes
gleamed. 'Oh, this is wonderful, isn't it, Ben? Sandy
will bring magic to Dolphin Bay. I just know it!'

Ben watched the tiny metallic particles as they
glistened on the white hospital sheets. Saw the pleasure in his aunt's shrewd gaze, the gleam of reluctant laughter in Sandy's eyes.

'Magic? Well, it *did* come from my fairy notebook,' she said.

Something called him to join in their complicity,
to believe in their fantasy.

Hope he'd thought long extinguished struggled to

revive itself. Magic? *Was* it magic that Sandy had brought with her? Magic from the past? Magic for the future? He desperately wanted to believe that.

But there was no such thing as magic. He'd learnt that on a violently blazing day five years ago, when he had been powerless to save the lives of his family.

He would need a hell of a lot more than some so-called fairy dust to change his mind.

CHAPTER SEVEN

THE FIRST THING Sandy noticed on the beach early the next morning was the dog. A big, shaggy golden retriever, it lay near a towel on the sand near the edge of the water with its head resting on its paws. Its gaze was directed out to the surf of Big Ray Beach, the beach she'd reached via the boardwalk from the bay.

Twelve years ago she'd thought 'Big Ray' must refer to a person. No. Ben had informed her the beach had another name on the maps. But the locals had named it after the two enormous manta rays that lived on the northern end of the beach and every so often undulated their way to the other end. He had laughed at her squeals and hugged her close, telling her they were harmless and that he would keep her safe from anything that dared hurt her.

This morning there were only a few people in the water; she guessed one of them must be the dog's owner. At six-thirty, with strips of cloud still tinged pink from sunrise, it was already warm, the weather gearing up for sultry heat after the previous day's storm. Cicadas were already tuning up their chorus for the day.

Sandy smiled at the picture of doggy devotion. *Get dog of own once settled in Melbourne,* she added in a mental memo for her 'to do' list. That-Jerk-Jason had allergies and wouldn't tolerate a dog in the house. How had she been so in love with him when they'd had so little in common apart from their jobs?

She walked up to the dog and dropped to her knees in the sand. She offered it her hand to sniff, then ruffled the fur behind its neck. 'Aren't you a handsome boy?' she murmured.

The dog looked up momentarily, with friendly, intelligent eyes, thumped his plumed tail on the sand, then resumed his vigil.

She followed the animal's gaze, curious to see the object of such devotion. The dog's eyes were fixed on a man who was body-surfing. His broad, powerful shoulders and athletic physique were in perfect sync with the wave, harnessing its energy as it curled behind him and he shot towards shore.

The man was Ben.

She knew that even before he lifted his head from the water, a look of intense exhilaration on his face as he powered down the face of the wave. He was as at home on a wave as he had been when he was nineteen, and for a moment it was as if she were thrown back into the past. So much of her time with him that summer had been spent on this beach.

She was transported back to a morning like this

when she'd run from the guesthouse to the sand and found him riding a wave, accompanied by a pod of dolphins, their grey shapes distinct on the underside of the wave. Joy and wonder had shone from his face. She'd splashed in to meet him and shared a moment of pure magic before the pod took off. Afterwards they'd lain on their backs on the beach, holding hands, marvelling over the experience. Did he remember?

Now he had seen her watching, and he lifted off the wave as it carried him into shore. She wanted to call out to him not to break off his ride on her account, but knew he wouldn't hear her over the sound of the surf.

He waved a greeting and swam, then strode towards her through the small breaking waves that foamed around his legs. Her breath caught in her throat at his near-naked magnificence. He was so tall and powerfully built that he seemed to dominate the vastness of the ocean and the horizon behind him.

His hair was dark and plastered to his head. The water was streaming off his broad shoulders and honed muscles. Sunlight glistened off the drops of water on his body so he seemed for one fanciful moment like some kind of mythical hero, emerging from the sea.

Desire, sudden and overwhelming, surged through her. Her nipples tensed and she seemed to melt inside. She wanted him. Longed for him. How could she ever have left him? She should have defied her parents and got back to Dolphin Bay. Somehow. Anyhow. Just to be with him.

That was back then. Now they were very different people who just happened to have found themselves on the same beach. But the attraction was as compelling as ever, undiluted by the years that had passed.

Why couldn't she forget that special time they had shared? What kept alive that fraction of hope that they could share it again? It wasn't just that she found him good-looking. This irrational compulsion was more than that. Something so powerful it overrode his rejection of her overtures. He didn't want her here. He had made that clear from the word go. She should just return his acquaintance-type wave and walk on.

But she ran in to the knee-deep waves to meet him. The dog splashed alongside her, giving a few joyous barks of welcome. She squealed at the sudden chill of the water as it sprayed her.

Remember, just friends, she reminded herself as she and Ben neared each other. Give him even a hint of the desire that had her so shaky and confused and he might turn back to that ocean and swim all the way to New Zealand.

'Good morning, Mr President,' she said. Ben as leader of the business community? It took some getting used to. And yet the air of authority was there when he dealt with his staff at the hotel—and they certainly gave him the deference due to a well-respected boss.

'Just Ben will do,' he said as he walked beside her onto the dry sand. As always, she had trouble keeping up with his stride.

She was finding it almost impossible not to look at his body, impressive in red board shorts. Kept casting sideways glances at him.

'So you've met Hobo,' he said, with an affectionate glance at the dog.

'No formal introductions were made, but we said hello,' she said, still breathless at her physical reaction to him. 'Is he yours?'

She felt self-conscious at Ben's nearness, aware that she was wearing only a bikini covered by the skimpiest of tank tops.

'My mother helps out at a dog shelter. Sometimes she brings dogs home to foster until they find permanent homes. This one clapped eyes on me, followed me to my house and has been with me ever since.' He leaned down to pat the dog vigorously. 'Can't get rid of you, can I, mate?' He spoke with ill-concealed affection.

So he had something to love.

She was glad.

'He's adorable. And he guarded your towel like a well-trained soldier.'

Ben picked up the towel from the sand and flung it around his neck. *How many times had she seen him do that in just the same way? How many times had he tucked his towel solicitously around her if her own towel was damp?*

'What brings you to the beach so early?' he asked.

She pulled a face. 'Had to walk those Snickers bars off.'

'How many gone?'

'Only two.'

'One for dinner and one for breakfast?'

'Chocolate for breakfast? I've got a sweet tooth, but I'm not a total sugar freak.' She scuffed her foot in the sand. 'I couldn't sleep. Kept thinking of all I don't know about managing a bookstore.' *Kept thinking about you.*

He picked up a piece of driftwood and threw it for Hobo. The dog bounded into the water to retrieve it.

'You took a lot of notes from Aunt Ida yesterday.'

'It's just nerves. Bay Books is so important for Ida and I want to get it right.'

'You'll be fine. It's only for a few days.'

No doubt he meant to sound reassuring. But it seemed as if he was reminding her yet again that he wanted her out of Dolphin Bay.

'Yes. Just a few days,' she echoed. 'I guess I won't bankrupt the place in that time.'

Hobo splashed out of the shallows with the driftwood in his mouth, grinning a doggy grin and looking very pleased with himself. He dropped it between their feet.

Sandy reached down to pick it up at the same time as Ben did. She collided with his warm, solid shoulders, felt her head connect with his. 'Ouch!' She rubbed the side of her temple.

'Are you okay?' Ben pulled her to her feet and turned her to face him.

They stood very close, her hands on his shoulders where she'd braced herself for balance. He was damp and salty and smelled as fresh and clean as the morning. It would be so easy to slide her hands down, to tangle her fingers in his chest hair, test the strength of his muscles. Every cell in her body seemed to tingle with awareness where his bare skin touched hers.

She nodded, scarcely able to speak. 'That's one tough skull you've got there. But I'm fine. Really.'

He gently probed her head, his fingers sending currents of sensation coursing through her. 'There's no bump.'

'I think I'll live,' she managed to choke out, desperately attempting to sound flippant.

His big scarred hands moved from her scalp to cradle her face. He tilted her head so she was forced to look up into his eyes. For a long moment he searched her face.

'I don't want to hurt you, Sandy,' he said, his voice hoarse.

She knew he wasn't talking about the collision. 'I realise that, Ben,' she whispered.

Then, with her eyes drowning in his, he kissed her.

She was so surprised she stood stock-still for a moment. Then she relaxed into the sensation of Ben's mouth on hers. It felt like coming home.

* * *

When Ben had lifted his head from the wave and had seen Sandy standing on the beach, it had been as if the past and the present had coalesced into one shining moment. A joy so unexpected it was painful had flooded his heart.

And here he was, against all resolutions, kissing her.

Her lips were warm and pliant beneath his. Her breasts were pressed to his chest. Her eyes, startled at first, were filled with an expression of bliss.

He shouldn't be kissing her. Starting things he could not finish. Risking pain for both of them. But those thoughts were lost in the wonder of having her close to him again.

It was as if the twelve years between kisses had never happened.

He twined his hands in her shiny vanilla-scented hair, tilted her head back as he deepened the kiss, pushed against her lips with his tongue. Her mouth parted to welcome him, to meet the tip of his tongue with hers.

She made a small murmur of appreciation and wound her arms around his neck. His arms slid to her waist, to the smooth, warm skin where her top stopped, drawing her close. He could feel her heart thudding against his chest.

He wanted her. She could surely feel his arousal. But this wasn't just about sex. It had always been so much more than that with Sandy.

The world shrank to just him and her, and the surf was a muted pounding that echoed the pulsing of their hearts, the blood running hot through his veins.

He could feel her nipples hard against him. Sensed the shiver of pleasure that vibrated through her. He pulled her tighter, wanting her as close to him as she could be.

But then something landed near his foot, accompanied by a piteous whining. Hobo. The driftwood. *Damn!*

He ignored it. Sand was dug in a flurry around them, stinging his legs. The whining turned to sharp, demanding barks.

Inwardly he cursed. Willed Hobo to go away. But the dog just kept on digging and barking. Ben broke away from the first time he'd kissed Sandy in twelve years for long enough to mutter, 'Get lost, boy.'

But when he quickly reclaimed Sandy's lips she was trembling. Not with passion but repressed laughter. 'He's not going to go away, you know,' she murmured against his mouth.

Ben groaned. He swore. He leaned down, grabbed the driftwood and threw it as far away as he could— so hard he nearly wrenched his shoulder.

Now Sandy was bent over with laughter. 'He wasn't going to let up, was he?'

Ben cursed his dog again.

'I know you don't really mean that,' she said, with a mischievous tilt to her mouth. 'Poor Hobo.'

'Back to the shelter for him,' Ben growled.

'As if,' said Sandy.

She looked up to him, her eyes still dancing with laughter. She looked as though she'd been thoroughly kissed. He didn't shave until after his morning surf and her chin was all pink from his beard. He felt a surge of possessiveness so fierce it was primal.

'That…that was nice, Ben.'

Nice? He struggled for a word to sum up what it had meant to him. When he didn't reply straight away, the soft, satisfied light of a woman who knew she was desired seemed to dim in her eyes.

'More than nice,' he said, and her eyes lit up again.

He reached out to smooth that wayward lock of hair from her eyes. She caught his hand with hers and dropped a quick kiss on it before she let it go.

'Why did you kiss me, Ben, when with every second breath you're telling me go away?'

Did he know the answer himself? 'Because I—'

He couldn't find the words to say, *Because you're Sandy, and you're beautiful, and I still can't believe you've come back to me, but I'm afraid to let you in because I don't want to love you and then lose you again.*

Her eyes were huge in her flushed face. She'd got damp from hugging him while he was still wet from the surf. Her tank top clung to her curves, her nipples standing erect through the layers of fabric.

She ran the edge of her pink pointy tongue along

her lips to moisten her mouth. He watched, fascinated, aching to kiss her again.

A tremor edged her voice. 'It's still there, isn't it, Ben? That attraction. That feeling there isn't anyone else in this world at this moment but you and me. It was like that from the start and it hasn't changed.' She took a deep gulp of air. 'If only...'

He clenched his fists so hard his scars ached. 'I told you—no if-onlys. That—the kiss—it shouldn't have happened.'

'Why not?' Her eyes were still huge. 'We're both free. Grown-up now and able to choose what we want from our lives, choose who we want to be with.'

Choose to leave when we want to.

Even after that one brief kiss he could feel what it would be like, having found her, to lose her again. He'd managed fine these past years on his own. He couldn't endure the pain of loss again.

She looked very serious, her brow creased. 'That time we had together all those years ago was so special. I don't know about you, but I was too young to appreciate just how special. I never again felt that certainty, that rightness. Maybe this unexpected time together is a gift. For us to get to know each other again. Or...or...maybe we have to try it again so that we can let it go. Have you thought of that?'

He shook his head. 'It's not that easy, Sandy.'

'Of course it isn't easy. It isn't easy for me either. I'm not in a rush to get my heart broken again.'

He noticed again the shadows under her eyes. Remembered her ex had got married yesterday. Typically, she wasn't letting on about her pain. But it was there.

'I can see that,' he said.

He was glad the beach was practically deserted, with just a few people walking along the hard, damp sand at the edge of the waves, others still in the surf. Hobo romped with another dog in the shallows.

Her voice was low and intense. 'Maybe if we gave it a go we'd…we'd burn it out.'

'You think so?' He couldn't keep the cynicism from his voice.

She threw up her hands. 'Who knows? After all this time we don't really know what the other is like now. Grown-up Sandy. Grown-up Ben. We might hate each other.'

'I can't see that happening.' Hate Sandy? No way. Never.

She scuffed the sand with her bare toes, not meeting his eyes. 'How do you know? I like to put a positive spin on things when I can. But, fact is, I haven't had a lot of luck with men. When I started dating—after I gave up on us seeing each other again—it seemed to me there were two types of men: nice ones, like you, who would ultimately betray me—'

He growled his protest.

She looked back up at him. 'I know now it was a misunderstanding between us, but I didn't know that then. If anyone betrayed me it was my father. By lying to me about you. By cheating on our family.'

He didn't disagree. 'And the second type of man?'

'Forceful, controlling guys—'

'Like your father?'

She nodded. 'They'd convince me they knew what was best for me. I'd be in too deep before I realised they had anything but my interests at heart. But obviously I must have been at fault, too, when things went wrong.'

'You're too hard on yourself.' He hated to see the tight expression on her face.

Her mouth twisted into an excuse of a smile. 'Am I? Even little things about a person can get annoying. Jason used to hate that I never replaced the empty toilet roll. It was only because the fancy holder he installed ruined my nails when I tried, but—'

Ben couldn't believe what he was hearing. 'What kind of a loser *was* this guy?'

'He wasn't a loser. He was smart. Clever. It seemed I could be myself with him. I thought at last I'd found Mr Perfect. But that was one of the reasons he gave for falling out of love with me.' She bit down hard on her lower lip. 'And he said I was noisy and a show-off.'

Ben was so astounded he couldn't find an appropriate response.

Her eyes flickered to his face and then away. 'When I first knew him he said I lit up a room just by coming into it. *Effervescent* was the word he used. By the end he said I embarrassed him with my loud behaviour.'

Her voice was forcedly cheerful but there was a catch to it that tore at Ben.

'But you don't want to hear about that.'

Anger against this unknown man who had hurt Sandy fuelled him. 'You're damn right I don't. It's crap. That jerk was just saying that to make himself feel better about betraying you.'

She pulled a self-deprecating face. 'I tell myself that too. It made me self-conscious around people for a while—you know…the noisy show-off thing. I couldn't help wondering if people were willing me to shut up but were too polite to say so. But…but I've put it behind me.'

With his index finger he tilted her face upwards. 'Sandy. Look at me. I would never, ever think you were an embarrassing show-off. I never have and I never will. Okay? You're friendly and warm and you put people at ease. That's a gift.'

'Nice of you to say so. Kind words are always welcome.' Her voice made light of what she said.

'And I would never give a damn about a toilet roll.'

Her mouth twitched. 'It sounds so dumb when you say it out loud. A toilet roll.' The twitch led to a smile and then to full-blown giggles. 'What a stupid thing for a relationship to founder over.'

'And what a moron he was to let it.'

Ben found himself laughing with her. It felt good.

Again, like oil on those rusty, seized emotions he had thought would never be kick-started into life again.

'I was just using the toilet roll as an example of how little things about a person can get annoying to someone else,' she said. Her laughter died away. 'After a few days of my company you might be glad to see the end of me.'

'And vice-versa?' The way he'd cut himself off from relationships, she was more likely to get the worst end of the bargain. He was out of the habit of being a boyfriend.

She nodded. 'Then we could both move on, free of…free of this thing that won't let go of us. With… with the past washed clean.'

'Maybe,' he conceded.

She wanted to rekindle old embers to see if they burned again or fizzled away into lifeless ash. But what if they raged away like a bush fire out of control and he was the one left scorched and lifeless? *Again.*

She took hold of his arm. Her voice was underscored with urgency. 'Ben, we should grab this second chance. Otherwise we might regret it for the rest of our lives. Like I regret that I didn't trust in what we had. I should have come back to you to Dolphin Bay. I was eighteen years old, for heaven's sake, not eight. What could my parents have done about it?'

'I came looking for you in Sydney.' He hadn't meant to let that out. Had never intended to tell her.

Her brows rose. 'When?'

'A few months after you left.'

'I didn't know.'

'You wouldn't. My mates were playing football at Chatswood, on the north shore. I had my dad's car to drive down with them.' He'd been up from university for the Easter break. 'After the game I found your place.'

'The house in Killara?'

He nodded. It had been a big house in a posh northern suburb, designed to show off her father's social status. 'I parked outside, hoping I'd see you. Not sure what I'd do if I did.'

'Why didn't you come in?'

'I was nineteen. You hadn't written. Or phoned. For all I knew you'd forgotten all about me. And I knew your father wouldn't welcome me.'

'Was I there? I can't believe while you were outside I might have been in my room. Probably sobbing into my diary about how much I was missing you.'

'Your hat was hanging on the veranda. I could see it from outside. That funny, stripy bucket hat you used to wear.'

She screwed up her face. 'I remember... I lost that hat.'

'No, you didn't. I took it. I jumped over the fence and snatched it.'

Her eyes widened. 'You're kidding me? My old hat? Do...do you still have it?'

'Once I was back in the car my mates grabbed it from me. When we crossed the Sydney Harbour Bridge they threw it out of the window.'

'Hey! That hat cost a whole lot of hard-earned babysitting money.'

She pretended outrage, but he could tell she was shaken by his story.

'I didn't steal it to see it squashed by a truck. I wanted to punch my mates out. But they told me to stop bothering with a girl who didn't want me when there were plenty who did.'

Sandy didn't say anything for a moment. Then she sighed. 'Oh, Ben, if only…' She shook her head. 'I won't say it. You're right. No point.'

'That's when I gave up on you.'

He'd said enough. He could never admit that for years afterwards when he'd driven over that spot on the bridge he'd looked out for her hat.

'And there *were* other girls?' She put her hand up in her halt sign. 'No. Don't tell me about them. I couldn't bear it.' Her eyes narrowed. 'I used to imagine all those blonde surfer chicks. Glad the city interloper was gone. Able to have their surf god all to themselves again.'

He stared at her incredulously. 'Did you just call me a surf god?'

Colour stained her cheeks. 'Hey, I'm in advertising. I get creative with copy.' But when she looked up at him her eyes were huge and sincere. 'I adored you, Ben. You must know that.' Her voice caught in her throat.

Ben shifted from foot to foot in the sand. 'I... Uh... Same here.' *He'd planned his life around her.*

'Let's spend these four days together,' she urged. 'Forget all that's happened to us since we last saw each other. Just go back to how we were. Sandy and Ben. Teenagers again. Carefree. Enjoying each other's company. Recapturing what we had.'

'You mean a fling?'

'A four-day fling? No strings? Why not? I'm prepared to risk it if you are.'

Risk. Was he ready to risk the safe life he'd so carefully constructed around himself in Dolphin Bay? He'd done so well in business by taking risks. But taking this risk—even for four days—could have far greater complications than monetary loss.

'Sandy. I hear what you're saying. But I need time.'

'Ben, we don't have time. We—'

Hobo skidded at their feet, the driftwood in his mouth, wet and eager and demanding attention.

Sandy glared at the animal. 'You have a great sense of timing, dog.'

'Yeah, he's known for it.' Ben reached down for the driftwood and tossed it just a short distance away. 'I've got to get him back. Dogs are only allowed unleashed on the beach before seven a.m.'

'And you can't be seen to be breaking the rules, can you?'

Was she taunting him?

No. The expression in her eyes was wistful, and he realised how she'd put herself on the line for him. For them. Or the possibility of them.

He turned to her. 'I'll consider what you said, Sandy.'

Her tone was again forcedly cheerful. 'Okay, Mr President.'

He grinned. 'I prefer surf god.'

'I'm going to regret telling you I called you that, aren't I? Okay, surf god. But don't take too long. These four days will be gone before we know it and then I'm out of here. Let's not waste them.' She turned to face the water. 'Are the mantas still in residence?'

'Yes. More likely their descendants, still scaring the hell out of tourists.'

He remembered how she'd started off being terrified of the big black rays. But by the end of that summer she'd been snorkelling around them. She had overcome her fears. Could he be as brave?

She reached up and hugged him. Briefly, he held her bare warmth to him before she pushed him away.

'Go,' she said, her voice not quite steady. 'Me? I'm having my first swim at Big Ray Beach for twelve years. I can't wait to get into the surf.'

With unconscious grace she pulled off her skimpy tank top, giving him the full impact of her body in a brief yellow bikini. *Her breasts were definitely bigger than they'd been when she was eighteen.*

Was he insane not to pull her back into his arms? To kiss her again? To laugh with her again? To have her as part of his life again?

For four days.

She headed for the water, treating him to a tantalising view of her sexy, shapely bottom. 'Come see me when you've done your thinking,' she called over her shoulder, before running into the surf.

She squealed as the cold hit her. Water sprayed up over her slim brown legs and the early sunlight shattered into a million glistening crystals. *More fairy dust.*

He looked at the tracks her feet had made in the sand. After the fire he had felt as if he'd been broken down to nothing—like rock into sand. Slowly, painfully, he had put himself back together. But there were cracks, places deep inside him, that still crumbled at the slightest touch.

If he let it, could Sandy's magic help give him the strength to become not the man he had been but someone better, finer, forged by the tragedy he had endured? Or would she break him right back down to nothing?

CHAPTER EIGHT

EVERY TIME THE old-fashioned bell on the top of the entrance door to Bay Books jangled Sandy looked up, heart racing, body tensed in anticipation. And every time it wasn't Ben she felt so let down she had to force herself to smile and cheerfully greet the customers, hoping they wouldn't detect the false note to her voice.

When would he come? Surely he wanted to be with her as much as she ached to be with him?

Or was he staying away because she had driven him away, by coming on too strong before he was ready? His reaction had both surprised and hurt her. Why had he been so uncertain about taking this second, unexpected chance with her? It was only for four days. Surely they could handle that?

She knew she should stop reliving every moment on the beach this morning over and over again, as if she were still eighteen. But she couldn't stop thinking about the kiss. That wonderful, wonderful kiss. After all those years it could have been a let-down. But kissing Ben again had been everything she had ever fantasised about. In his arms, his mouth claiming hers, she'd still felt the same heady mix of comfort, pleasure and bone-melting desire. It was as if their twelve-year separation had never happened.

Although there was a difference. Now she wanted him with an adult's hunger—an adult's sensual knowledge of the pleasures that could follow a kiss.

She remembered how on fire with first-time desire she'd felt all that time ago, when they'd been making out behind the boat shed. Or in the back seat of his father's car, parked on the bluff overlooking the ocean. They hadn't even noticed the view. Not that they could have seen it through the fogged-up windows.

And yet she hadn't let him go all the way. Hadn't felt ready for that final step. Even though she had been head-over-heels in love with him.

Her virginal young self hadn't appreciated the effort it must have taken for Ben to hold back. 'When you're ready,' he'd always said. Not like her experiences with boys in Sydney—'suitable' sons of her fathers' friends—all grabby hands and then sulks when she'd slapped them away. No. Ben truly had been her Sir Galahad on a surfboard.

Would a four-day fling include making love with Ben? That might be more than she—or Ben—could handle. They should keep it to kissing. And talking. And lots of laughing. Like it had been back then. Carefree. Uncomplicated.

She refused to listen to that nagging internal

voice. *Could anything be uncomplicated with the grown-up Ben?*

She forced her thoughts back to the present and got on with her work. She had to finish the job Ida had been in the middle of when she'd fallen—unpacking a delivery and slotting the books artfully onto the 'new releases' table.

Just minutes later, with a sigh of satisfaction, she stepped back to survey her work. She loved working in the bookshop. Even after just a few hours she felt right at home. The individuality and quirkiness of Ida's set-up connected with her, though she could immediately see things she'd like to change to bring the business model of this bricks-and-mortar bookstore more in step to compete with the e-bookstores. That said, if she could inject just a fraction of Bay Books' charm into her candle shop she'd be very happy. She must write in her fairy notebook: *Ask Ida about Balinese woodcarvers.*

But it wasn't just about the wooden dolphins with their enchanting carved smiles. The idyllic setting was a vital part of Bay Books. Not, she suspected, to be matched by the high-volume-retail-traffic Melbourne mall the candle people would insist on for their shop. It might be hard to get as excited about that.

Here, she only had to walk over to the window to view the quaint harbour, with the old-fashioned stone walls that sheltered it from the turquoise-blue waters of the open sea—only had to push the door open to hear the squawk of seagulls, breathe in the salt-tangy air.

This morning, in her hotel room, she had been awoken by a chorus of kookaburras. When she'd opened the sliding doors to her balcony it had been to find a row of lorikeets, the small, multi-coloured parrots like living gems adorning the balcony railing. On her way to the beach she'd surprised two small kangaroos, feeding in the grass in the bushland between the boardwalk and the sand dunes of Big Ray. It was good for the soul.

What a difference from fashionable, revitalised inner-city Surry Hills, where she lived in Sydney. It had more restaurants, bars and boutiques than she would ever have time to try. But it was densely populated and in summer could be stiflingly hot and humid. Driving round and round the narrow streets, trying to find somewhere to park her car, she'd sometimes dreamed of living in a place closer to nature.

And here she was back in Dolphin Bay, working in a stranger's bookshop, reconnecting with her first love.

It seemed surreal.

She paused, a paperback thriller in her hand. Remembered her pink-inked resolution. *Get as far away from Sydney as possible.*

That didn't necessarily have to mean moving to Melbourne.

But she had only ever been a city girl. Could she

settle for small-town life and the restrictions that entailed?

The bell sounded again. She looked up, heart thudding, mouth suddenly dry. But again it wasn't Ben. It was red-haired Kate, the waitress from the hotel.

'Hey, nice to see you, Kate,' she said, masking her disappointment that the woman wasn't her tall blond surf god.

'You too,' said Kate. 'We all love this shop and the personal service Ida gives us. It's great you're able to help her out.'

'Isn't it? I'm getting the hang of things. Can I help you with a book?' she asked.

Kate smiled and Sandy wondered if she could tell how inexperienced a shopkeeper she was.

'Ida ordered some titles for me, but in all the drama yesterday I didn't get a chance to see if they were in.'

'Sure,' said Sandy, heading behind the counter to access Ida's computer. She had the special orders file open when Kate leaned towards her over the carved wooden counter.

'So, I heard you and Ben were kissing on the beach this morning.'

Sandy was so flabbergasted she choked. She coughed and spluttered, unable to utter a word in response.

Kate rushed around the counter and patted Sandy's back until her breath came more easily.

'Thanks,' Sandy finally managed to choke out.

'Don't be so surprised. News travels fast in Dolphin Bay.'

Sandy took another ragged breath. 'I'm beginning to see that.'

Kate's green eyes gleamed. 'So you *were* kissing Ben?'

Again Sandy was too aghast to reply. 'Well, I…' she started.

'She who hesitates is thinking of how to tell me to mind my own business,' said Kate with a grin.

Sandy laughed at her audacity. 'Well, now that you mention it…'

'Feel free to tell me to keep my big mouth shut, but…well, I love Ben to pieces and I don't want—'

Ben and Kate?

Sandy felt dizzy—not from lack of air but from the feeling that her heart had plummeted to the level of her ballet flats. 'I'm sorry, Kate, I didn't know… He didn't say…'

Kate's auburn eyebrows rose. 'I don't mean *that* kind of love. My mum and Ben's mum are friends. I grew up with Ben. It's his brother, Jesse, I have a thing for. Unrequited, unfortunately.'

'Oh,' said Sandy, beyond relieved that Kate hadn't marched into the bookshop to stake a claim on Ben.

Kate leaned closer. 'You *do* realise that for Ben to be kissing a woman in public is a big, big deal?'

Sandy took a step back. 'It was six-thirty in the morning on a practically deserted beach.'

'That might be private in Sydney, but not in a place like Dolphin Bay. Here, it takes one person to see for everyone to know.'

'I had no idea.' Sandy felt suddenly dry in the mouth. What kind of pressure did this put on Ben? On her?

'You and Ben together is big news.'

'Then next time—if there is a next time—I'll make sure we're completely alone.'

She spoke with such vehemence that Kate frowned and took a step back from her. 'I'm sorry, Sandy. But this is a small town. We all look out for each other. If you're not serious about Ben don't start something you're not prepared to see through.'

Sandy gripped the edge of the counter. She knew Ben had been to hell and wasn't yet all the way back. She didn't need anyone to tell her.

Pointedly, she scrolled through the special orders file on Ida's computer, looked up again at Kate. 'I don't see your order here, but your contact number is. How about I call you when it comes in?'

Kate shifted from foot to foot. 'You must think I'm the nosiest busybody you've ever met.'

Sandy didn't disagree.

'But I've only got Ben's interests at heart,' Kate continued, sounding hurt.

Sandy gentled her tone of voice. 'I appreciate that.'

She was gratified at Kate's smile as she said goodbye. Despite the redhead's total lack of tact, she thought she could get to like her.

But Kate's visit, with her revelation about the undercurrents of small-town life, had left her reeling. She'd had no idea that any reunion would be conducted under such watchful eyes. What had seemed so simple on the beach at dawn suddenly seemed very complicated.

It made her self-conscious when dealing with the customers who came in dribs and drabs through the doors. Were they genuinely interested in browsing through the books—or in perusing her? Her doubts were realised when two older ladies, hidden from full view behind a display of travel books, spoke in too-loud whispers they obviously thought she couldn't hear.

'She seems nice, and Ida likes her,' said the first one. 'That's a point in her favour.'

Sandy held her breath when she realised they were talking about her.

'It might be a good thing. Ben's been in mourning for too long. His mother's worried about him,' said the other.

'I wonder what Jodi's parents will think.' The first lady sighed. 'Such a sweet girl. What a loss. No wonder Ben's stayed on his own all this time.'

Sandy slammed her hand over her mouth so the ladies wouldn't hear her gasp. *Jodi.* Ben's late wife. The gentle woman Ben had loved enough to marry and have a child with.

She stared ahead without seeing. Noticed a poster promoting a bestselling new celebrity biography had come adrift at one corner. But she felt too shaken to do anything about it. Would there always be the memory of another woman coming between her and Ben? *Could she cope with coming second? With being just a disposable fling while his wife always held first place in his heart?*

She couldn't meet the ladies' eyes when they scurried out through the door without buying a book.

An old familiar panic had started to overwhelm her—the same panic she'd used to feel when she'd been faced with those big waves rearing up so aggressively as she'd stood dry-mouthed with terror on the beach. Ben had helped her conquer that fear and discover the joy of riding the waves—and she'd used the memory to help her deal with any number of challenges she'd faced in her career. But now what she'd thought would be smooth water ahead might be filled with swirling undercurrents. Did she have the strength to battle through the rough water?

Was it worth it for a four-day fling?

The bell on the top of the door jangled again. She jumped. More ladies to check her out and assess her suitability?

Ben shouldered his way through the door, carrying two large take-away coffee containers. The smile he gave her made her heart do the flippy thing—backwards, forwards and tumbling over itself. Her breath seemed to accelerate, making her feel lightheaded, giddy.

Her surf god. In the flesh and hotter than ever.

He was back in shorts, and a blue polo shirt that hugged the breadth of his shoulders and brought out the blue of his eyes. She preferred the semi-naked beach look, but in true surf god manner he looked wonderful in anything he wore.

She smiled back in her joy at seeing him again. It was four hours and thirty-five minutes since she'd said goodbye to him on the beach.

She prayed no customers would intrude. More than ever she needed to be alone with Ben. To be re-assured that the thing between them was worth taking the risks of which she'd been so blithely ignorant.

Kate's words had hit home. Made her all too aware of the power she had to wound Ben. After all, she was the one who had left him all those years ago. Then he'd been young and untroubled, and still she had hurt him. Now he was anything but untroubled.

Could he deal with a walk-away-from-it fling?

Could *she*?

The expectations of her were frightening. But what if the reality of Ben didn't match up to her memories? What if they didn't have a thing in common and she wanted to run after the first twenty-four hours? What if he wanted her to stay and she hurt him all over again? Or if she fell hard for him again but couldn't match up to his wife? Then it would be her with her heart broken again.

She caught her breath in what felt dangerously like a sob.

Could she do this?

'You okay?'

His marvellous blue eyes were warm with concern for her. That sexy, sexy mouth was set in a serious line that just made her want to kiss it into a smile. Wordlessly, she nodded.

Could she not do it?

'Apparently we were seen on the beach this morning,' she said.

'Seen and duly noted. Makes you wonder what else people have to do with their time.'

'You're big news in Dolphin Bay.'

He put the coffee down on the counter. 'You're bigger news.'

'Tell me about it. The predatory city slicker hunting down the town's favourite son.'

She'd meant that to sound like a joke. But as soon as it came out she knew it was anything but funny.

Ben frowned. 'Did someone say that?'

'Yes. Well, not in so many words. Kate dropped in.' She couldn't help the wobble in her voice.

Why had Kate and those women come in and ruined everything? Made her feel suddenly so self-conscious with Ben?

She just wanted to fall back into his arms and continue where they'd left off this morning. But the exchange she'd overheard had unsettled her.

She bit down on her lower lip and looked up at Ben, not certain what to do next. How could she tell him she was having cold feet because she was so terrified of hurting him? Could she find the courage to ask him about Jodi?

CHAPTER NINE

To Ben, Sandy looked as if she'd always stood behind the counter of Bay Books. The short hair he was still getting used to was tucked behind her ears. Just below her left shoulder she had pinned a round metal badge that urged people to get involved with a local literacy campaign. She looked smart, efficient—every inch the professional salesperson. Yet her yellow dress seemed to bring the sunlight right into the corners of the dark wooden carvings so favoured by Aunt Ida, and her vanilla scent brought a sweet new warmth.

She fitted right in.

Ida would be delighted.

But Sandy looked anything but happy—she was wary, guarded, with a shadow behind her eyes. She was chewing her lip so hard she was in danger of drawing blood.

Fear gripped him deep in his gut. What gave here?

'Hey,' he said, and went around the counter to pull her into his arms, expecting her warm curves to relax against him. Instead she stiffened and resisted his embrace.

Why the sudden cold change? Hell, he'd worked damn hard to pull down a chink in those barriers he'd built up. Had she now decided to put up a few of her own?

It didn't figure.

'What's going on?' he asked.

Sandy took a step back, her struggle to decide what to tell him etched on her face. She picked up a waxed paper coffee cup, took a sip. Her hand wasn't quite steady and the froth on the top wobbled dangerously. She put it down and the foam slid over the lid of the cup and dribbled down its side.

'Leave it,' he said as she reached for a cloth to wipe it up.

'No. It might damage the wood,' she said.

She cleaned the spill too thoroughly. A delaying tactic if ever he'd seen one.

She put the cloth away, started to speak way too rapidly. 'Why don't we take our coffee over to the round table?' She was gabbling, her eyes blinking rapidly as she looked everywhere but at him. 'It's a cosier place to have coffee. Y'know, I'm thinking it would be great for Ida to have a café here. Maybe knock through to the vacant shop next door so that customers—'

She went to pick up the coffee cup again, but he closed his hand around her wrist to stop her. He wouldn't give her an excuse to evade him. Her hand stilled under his. 'Tell me. Now.'

Her eyes flickered up to meet his and then back down. When she spoke, her words came out in a rush. 'Kate told me the whole town is watching to see if I hurt you.'

In his relief, he cursed. 'Is that all?' He let go her wrist.

'What do you mean, *is that all*?' Hands on hips, she glared at him with the ferocity of a fluffed-up kitten. 'Don't you patronise me, Ben Morgan. Kate really freaked me out.'

He used both hands to push down in a gesture of calm. 'Kate exaggerates. Kate and the old-school people who were here before Dolphin Bay became a hotspot for escapees from the city. They all mind each other's business.'

Sandy's chin tilted upwards. 'And your business in particular, if Kate's to be believed.'

He shook his head. 'It's no big deal.'

'Are you telling me that's part and parcel of living in a small town?'

He picked up his coffee. Drank a few mouthfuls to give him time to think. It was just as he had predicted. *Ben's old girlfriend is back.* He could practically hear the hot news humming through cyberspace. 'Yeah. Better get used to it.'

'I don't know if I can.' Her voice rose to a higher pitch. 'I'm used to the don't-give-a-damn attitude of the city.'

Ben thought back to how the town had pulled together for him after the fire. How it had become so stifling he'd had to get away. He'd thrown himself into high-risk money-making ventures because he'd had nothing to lose when he'd already lost everything. They'd paid off in spades. And he'd come back. Dolphin Bay would always be home. No matter that sad memories haunted him at every turn.

But why should that hothouse concern for him bother Sandy?

Her arms were crossed defensively against her chest. Was she using her fear of the townfolk's gossip to mask some deeper reluctance? Some concern she had about him?

He chose his words carefully. 'I can see that. But you're only here for four more days. We're not thinking beyond that, right? Why worry about what they think?'

'I just do,' she said, in a very small voice.

He put down his coffee, put his finger under her chin and tilted it upwards so she was forced to meet his gaze. 'What else did Kate say?'

'It wasn't Kate. There were some other women. Customers. They…they were talking about…about Jodi.'

Pain knifed through him at the sound of Jodi's name. People tended to avoid saying it in front of him.

His feelings must have shown on his face, because Sandy looked stricken.

'Ben, I'm so sorry…'

She went to twist away from him, but he stopped her.

'I should tell you about Jodi.'

The words would be wrenched from him, but he had to tell Sandy about his wife. There should be no secrets between them. Not if they were to enjoy the four days they had together.

'Ben. No. You don't have to—'

He gently put his hand over her mouth to silence her and she nodded.

He dropped his hand. 'I loved Jodi. Don't ever think otherwise. She was a good wife and a wonderful mother.'

'Of course.' Sandy's eyes were warm with compassion—and a touch of wariness.

'I'd known her all my life. But I didn't date her until I'd finished university and was working in Melbourne.'

Sandy's brows rose. 'University? You said—'

'You wouldn't catch me in a classroom again?'

'That's right. You said it more than once. I remember because I was looking forward to going to uni.'

'You can thank your father for my business degree.'

She frowned. 'My father? I—'

'He used to look at me as if I were something scraped off the bottom of his shoe. Left me in no doubt that I wasn't worthy of his daughter.' Ben would have liked to apply some apt swear words to his memories of Dr Randall Adams, but Sandy might not appreciate that.

Sandy protested. 'Surely he didn't say that to you? I can't believe he—'

'He didn't have to say it. I saw his sneer.'

Her mouth twisted. 'No wonder I never got your letters.'

Teen testosterone had made him want to flatten the guy. 'But he had a point. To be worthy of his daughter I needed to get off my surfboard and make something of myself. I had deferred places at universities in both Sydney and Melbourne to choose from.'

'You never said…'

'At the time I had no intention of taking either. I just wanted to surf every good break at Big Ray Beach and work for my dad when I needed money to travel to other surf beaches. That summer… I guess it made me grow up.'

He'd been determined to prove Dr Adams wrong. And broadening his horizons had been the right choice, even if made for the wrong reasons. And now fate had brought Sandy back to him. Now they met as equals in every way.

'You could have been studying at the same uni as me,' Sandy said slowly. She pulled a face that looked sad rather than funny. 'I won't say *if only* again.'

They both fell silent. But Ben refused to give in to musing about what might have been. He had tortured himself enough.

Sandy cleared her throat. 'What happened after you finished uni?'

'I was offered a job in a big stockbroking firm in Melbourne. Got an apartment and stayed down there.'

'But you came home for holidays? And…and met up with Jodi again?'

He could tell Sandy was finding the conversation awkward. She twisted the fabric of her skirt between the fingers of her right hand without seeming to be aware she was doing it.

'I had an accident in the surf. Got hit in the face with the fin of my board.' His hand went to the scar on his lip. 'Jodi was the nurse who looked after me at the hospital.'

And it had started from there. A relaxed, no-strings relationship with a sweet, kind-hearted girl that had resulted in an unplanned pregnancy.

He'd said there were to be no secrets from Sandy, but Liam's unexpected conception was something he didn't want to share with her. Not yet. Maybe never.

'Jodi moved down to Melbourne with me after we got married.'

'What…what brought you both back to Dolphin Bay?'

'I'm not a city guy. I'd had it with Melbourne. The insane work hours, the crowds, the traffic. Mum and Dad were tired of running the guesthouse. Jodi wanted to be with family when she had the baby.'

He gritted his teeth, trying not to let himself be

overwhelmed by emotion when he thought of his baby son. The son he'd loved so fiercely from the moment he'd been placed in his arms as a newborn and yet hadn't been able to protect.

'I could trade shares from here. Start business projects here.'

There was another pause. Sandy twisted the edge of her skirt even tighter. 'Those ladies… They…they said Jodi's parents wouldn't be happy with me coming onto the scene.'

Ben clenched his hands into fists. Who *were* these busybody troublemakers? If he found out he'd tell them to damn well butt out of his business.

He shook his head. 'Not true. Jodi's mum and dad are good people. They want me to…to have someone in my life again.'

Sandy's eyes widened. 'You know that for sure?'

'Yes. They've told me not to let the…the tragedy ruin my life. That…that it's not what Jodi would have wanted.'

'And you believe that? About Jodi?'

He nodded. His words were constricted in his throat. 'The night Liam was born she told me that if anything happened to her—she was a nurse and knew there could be complications in childbirth—she didn't want me to be on my own. She…she made me promise I would find someone else…'

'Oh, Ben.'

Sandy laid her hand on his arm. He realised she

was close to tears. When she spoke again her voice was so choked he had to strain to hear her.

'How can I live up to such a wonderful woman?'

In a few shaky steps she made her way around the counter and stood with her back to him. She picked up a book from the display and put it back in exactly the same place.

'Sandy, it isn't a competition.'

Her voice was scarcely a murmur. 'There would always be a third person in our relationship. I don't know that I could deal with that…'

'Sandy, didn't you hear what I said? Jodi would *want* me to take this chance to spend time with you.'

She turned to face him, the counter now a barrier between them. Her eyes, shadowed again, searched his face. 'Jodi sounds like…like an angel.'

Ben forced himself to smile through the pain. 'She'd laugh to hear you say that. Jodi *was* special, and I loved her. But she was just a human being, like the rest of us, with her own strengths and weaknesses.'

'Ben, I'm no angel either. Don't expect me to be. I'm quick to make judgements, grumpy when I'm hungry or tired—and don't dare to cross me at my time of the month. Oh, and there's the toilet roll thing.'

Despite the angst of talking about Jodi, Sandy made him smile. Just as she'd done when she was eighteen. 'You can let me deal with that.'

She pushed the hair away from her forehead in

a gesture of weariness. 'I…I don't know that I've thought this through very well.'

'What do you mean?' he asked.

Fear knifed him again.

He'd had five major turning points in his life. One when he'd decided to go to university. The second when he'd married Jodi. The third when Liam was born. Fourth, the fire. And the fifth when he'd looked up from that wave this morning and seen Sandy standing on the shore next to his dog, as if she were waiting for him to come home to her.

Since he'd kissed her he'd thought of nothing but Sandy. Of the impact she'd made in less than twenty-four hours on his safe, guarded, ultimately sterile life.

He hadn't wanted her here. But her arrival in town had forced him to take stock. And what he saw was a bleak, lonely future—a half-life—if he continued to walk the solitary path he had mapped for himself. He had grieved. A part of him would always grieve. But grief that didn't heal could twist and turn and fester into something near madness—if he let it.

He would *not* allow Sandy to back away from him now. She'd offered four days and he was going to take them.

She took a deep breath. 'The you-and-me thing. What if it doesn't work out and I…and I hurt you again? You've endured so much. I couldn't bear it if I caused you more pain.'

'Leave that to me. It's a gamble I'll take.'

Sandy was his best bet for change. The ongoing power of his attraction to her improved the odds. Her warmth, her vivacity, made him feel as though the seized-up machinery that was his heart was slowly grinding back to life.

She gave him hope.

Maybe that was her real magic—a magic that had nothing to do with shop-bought fairy glitter.

There were four more days until she had to leave for Melbourne. He didn't know what he brought to the table for *her* in terms of a relationship. But he'd be a fool not to grab the second chance she'd offered him. No matter the cost if he lost her again.

'Are you still worried about the townsfolk? They're nothing to be scared of.'

She set her shoulders, tossed back her head. 'Scared? Who said I'm scared?' Her mouth quirked into the beginnings of a smile. 'Maybe…maybe I *am* a little scared.'

Scared of him? Was that the real problem? Was she frightened he would rush her into something before she was ready?

He ached to make love to Sandy. Four days might not be enough to get to that stage. But he could wait if that was what she needed. Even though the want, the sheer physical ache to possess her, was killing him.

'No need to be. I'm here to fight battles for you. Never forget that.'

At last her smile reached her eyes. 'You're sure about that?'

She looked so cute he wanted to kiss the tip of her nose.

He stepped around the counter towards her at the same time she moved towards him. He took both her hands in his and pulled her to him. This time she didn't resist. Her face was very close. That warm vanilla scent of hers was already so familiar.

'As sure as I am about taking that second chance we've been offered. Let's give it everything we've got in the next four days. Turn back the clock.'

She stared at him. He couldn't blame her for being surprised at his turnaround. The shadow behind her eyes was not completely gone. Had she told him everything that was worrying her?

'Are you serious?' she choked out.

'Very.'

She reached up her hand to stroke the side of his cheek. As if checking he was real. When it came, her smile was tender and her eyes were warm. 'I'm so happy to hear you say that. It's just that…' She paused

'What?' he asked.

'All these expectations on us. It…it's daunting. And what will we tell people?'

'Nothing. Let them figure it out for themselves.' He gripped her hands. 'This is just about you and me. It's always just been you and me.'

'And we—'

'Enough with the talking,' he growled, and he silenced her with a kiss.

A kiss to seal their bargain. A kiss to tell her what words could not.

But the kiss rapidly escalated to something hot and hungry and urgent. She matched his urgency with lips, teeth, tongue. He let go her hands so he could pull her tight. Her curves shaped to him as though they were made to fit and she wound her arms around his neck to pull him closer. The strap of her yellow dress slid off her shoulder. He wanted to slide the dress right off her.

He broke away from the kiss, his breath hard and ragged. 'We're out of here. To get some privacy.'

'Wh…what about the shop?' Her own ragged breathing made her barely coherent.

'How many books have you sold today?'

'Just…just a few.'

'Yeah. Not many customers. Too many gossips.' He stroked the bare warm skin on her shoulder, exalted in her shiver of response.

'They did seem to spend more time lurking around corners and looking at me than browsing,' she admitted.

Her hands slid through his hair with an unconscious sensuality that made him shudder with want.

'You shut down the computer. I'll set the alarm.'

'But Ida…'

'Don't worry about Ida.' He could easily make up to his aunt for any drop in sales figures.

Sandy started to say something. He silenced her with another kiss. She moaned a throaty little sound that made him all the more determined to get her out of here and to somewhere private, where he could kiss her without an audience.

The old-fashioned doorbell on the top of the shop door jangled loudly.

Sandy froze in his arms. Then she pulled away from him, cheeks flushed, eyes unfocused. Her quiet groan of frustration echoed his. She pressed a quick, hard kiss on his mouth and looked up wordlessly at him.

To anyone coming into the store they would look as guilty as the pair of teenagers they'd once been. He rolled his eyes. Sandy started to shake with repressed giggles.

He kept his arm firmly around her as they turned to face the two middle-aged women who had entered the shop. Both friends of his mother.

Two sets of eyebrows had risen practically to their hairlines.

News of kiss number two for the day would be rapidly telegraphed through the town.

And he didn't give a damn.

'Sorry, ladies,' he said, in a voice that put paid to any argument. 'This shop is closed.'

CHAPTER TEN

DESTINATION? SOMEWHERE THEY could have privacy. Purpose? To talk more freely about what had happened to each other in the twelve years since she'd left Dolphin Bay. And Sandy didn't give a flying fig that the two bemused ladies Ben had ousted from Bay Books stood hands on hips and watched as she and Ben hastened away from the shop.

Even just metres down the street she fell out of step with Ben and had to skip to catch up. He turned to wait for her, suppressed laughter still dancing around his mouth, and extended his hand for her to take.

Sandy hesitated for only a second before she slid her fingers through his. Linked hands would make quite a statement to the good folk of Dolphin Bay. Anticipation and excitement throbbed through her as he tightened his warm, strong grip and pulled her closer. She smiled up at him, her breath catching in her throat at his answering smile.

When she'd very first held hands with Ben the simple act had been a big deal for her. Most of her schoolfriends had already had sex with their boy-friends by the age of eighteen. Not her. She'd never met a boy she'd wanted to do more with than kiss. When she'd met Ben she'd still been debating the significance of hands held with just palms locked or, way sexier, with fingers entwined.

And Ben?

Back then he'd had no scars.

'Where are we going?' she asked, surprised when her voice came out edged with nervousness.

'My place,' he said. His voice didn't sound nervous in the slightest.

Did he live at the hotel? That would make sense. Maybe in an apartment as luxurious as the room where she was staying.

'Do you remember my family's old boathouse?' he asked as he led her down the steps in front of the hotel.

'Of course I do,' she said, and she felt herself colour. Thirty years old and blushing at the memory of that ramshackle old boathouse. Dear heaven, she hoped he didn't notice.

On the sand outside the boathouse, in the shelter of Ben's father's beached dinghies, she and Ben had progressed from first base to not-ready-to-progress-further-than-third.

She glanced quickly up at Ben. Oh, yes, he remembered too. The expression in those deep blue eyes made that loud and clear.

She blushed a shade pinker and shivered at the

memory of all that thwarted teen sexuality—and at the thought of how it might feel to finally do something about it if she and Ben got to that stage this time around.

'I live in the boathouse,' he said.

'You *live* there?' She didn't know what else to say that would not come out sounding ill-mannered.

Instead, she followed Ben across the sand in silence, wondering why a successful businessman would choose to live in something that was no more than a shack.

But the structure that sat a short distance to the right of the hotel bore little resemblance to the down-at-heel structure of her memory. Like so much of Dolphin Bay, it had changed beyond recognition.

'Wow! I'm impressed,' she said.

Ben's remodelled boathouse home looked like something that could star on a postcard. Supported by piers on the edge of the bay, its dock led out into the water. Timber-panelled walls were weathered to a silvery grey in perfect harmony with the corrugated iron of the peaked roof. Window trim and carriage lamps had been picked out in a deep dusky blue. Big tubs of purple hydrangeas in glazed blue pots sat either side of the door.

Ben leaned down to pluck a dead leaf from one of the plants without even seeming to realise he did it. She wouldn't have taken him for a gardener—but then she knew so very little of what interests he might have developed in the years since they'd last been together at this rich-in-memories part of the beach.

'The boathouse was the only part of the guest-house to survive the fire,' Ben said. He pushed open the glossy blue door. 'Jesse lived here before he went away. I had it remodelled as guest accommodation, but liked it so much I kept it for myself.'

'I can see why,' she said. 'I envy you.'

A large ceramic dog bowl filled with water, hand-painted with the words 'Hobo Drinks Here', sat just outside the door. She remembered the look of devotion in the dog's big eyes and Ben's obvious love for him.

'Where's your adorable dog?' she asked, stepping through the door he held open for her, fully expecting the retriever to give Ben a boisterous greeting.

'Mum dog-sits him the days I can't take him to work with me,' he said. 'Seems she always has a houseful of strays. He fits right in.'

Sandy was about to say something about his mother, but the words were stopped by her second, 'Wow!' as Ben stepped aside and she got her first glimpse of the interior of the boathouse.

She only had a moment to take in a large open-plan space, bleached timber and shades of white, floor-to-ceiling windows facing the water at the living room end and a vast wooden bed at the other.

The thought that it would be a fabulous location for an advertising shoot barely had time to register in her mind, because the door slammed shut behind them and she was in Ben's arms.

Ben didn't want to give a tour of the boathouse. He didn't want to talk about the architectural work Jesse had done on the old building. He just wanted, at last, to have Sandy to himself.

For a long, still moment he held her close, his arms wrapped tightly around her. He closed his eyes, breathed in the vanilla scent of her hair, scarcely able to believe it was real and she was here with him. He could feel the warm sigh of her breath on his neck, hear the thud-thud-thud of her heartbeat. Then he kissed her. He kissed the curve of her throat. He kissed the delicate hollow beneath her ear. He pressed small, hungry kisses along the line of her jaw. Then he kissed her on the mouth.

Without hesitation Sandy kissed him right back. She tasted of coffee and chocolate and her own familiar sweetness. As she wound her arms around his neck, met his tongue with hers, she made that sexy little murmur deep in her throat that he remembered from a long time ago. It drove him nearly crazy with want.

Secure in the privacy of the boathouse, he kissed her long enough for them to catch right up on the way they'd explored kissing each other all those years ago. Until kissing no longer seemed enough.

The straps of her yellow dress gave little resistance as he slid them down her smooth shoulders.

She shrugged to make it easier for him. Without the support of the straps, the top of her dress fell open. He could see the edge of her bra, the swell of her breasts, the tightness of her nipples. He kissed down her neck and across the roundness of her breasts, until she gasped and her hands curled tightly into his shoulders.

He couldn't get enough of her.

But with an intense effort he forced himself to pull back. 'Do you want me to stop?'

'No,' she said immediately. 'Not yet. I couldn't bear it if you stopped.'

In reply, he scooped her up into his arms. Her eyes widened with surprise and excitement. Her arms tightened around his neck and she snuggled her cheek against his shoulder.

She laughed as he marched her towards the bedroom end of the boathouse. 'Even more muscles than when you were nineteen,' she murmured in exaggerated admiration, her voice husky with desire.

She was still laughing as he laid her on the bed—his big, lonely bed. Her dress was rucked up around her slender tanned thighs, giving him a tantalising glimpse of red panties. She kicked off her shoes into the air, laughed again as they fell to the wooden floor with two soft thuds. Then she held out her arms to urge him to join her. Warm, vibrant Sandy, just as he remembered her. Only more womanly, more confident, more seductive.

He kicked off his own shoes and lay down next to

her. He leaned over her as she lay back against the pillows, her face flushed, her eyes wide.

'I never thought I'd see you back here.' His voice was hoarse with need for her.

She kissed him. 'Do you remember the sand outside this place? How scratchy it was?' she asked. 'How we'd sneak off there whenever we could get away from everyone.'

'How could I forget?' he replied. Ever since she'd walked into the hotel and back into his life he'd thought of little else.

'This is so much more comfortable,' she said, with on-purpose seduction in her smile. She pulled him down to her to kiss him again. 'And private,' she murmured against his mouth.

Her kiss was urgent, hungry, and he responded in kind. Outside on that sand as teenagers they'd fooled around as though they had all the time in the world. Now they had a clock ticking on their reunion. And they were playing grown-up games.

Within minutes he'd rid her of her dress and her bra. He explored the lush new fullness of her breasts. Kissed and teased her nipples.

He lifted his head and she made a murmur of protest. His voice was ragged. 'You sure you're ready for this?'

Sandy's eyes were huge. 'I should say no. I should say we need to spend more time together first, that we can't rush into anything we might regret.' Her voice broke. 'But I can't say no. I want you too much.

Have always wanted you… Don't stop, Ben. Please don't stop.'

What she'd said about not rushing made sense. This was going faster than he could have anticipated. He should be the sensible one. Should stop it. But he was beyond thinking sensibly when it came to Sandy. *He only had four days with her.*

She kissed him. He kissed her back and was done for. The last restraints gone. He stroked down the curve of her belly, felt her tremble at his touch. Then her panties were gone and he explored there too.

'Not fair. I want to get you naked as well,' she murmured as she started to divest him of his clothes.

She kissed a hot trail across his chest as she slid off his shirt, stroked right down his arms. Her fingers weren't quite steady as she fumbled with the zipper on his shorts. It made the act of pulling them over his hips a series of tantalising caresses along his butt and thighs that made his body harden so much it ached.

Then they were naked together.

Sandy's heart was doing the flipping over thing so rapidly she felt dizzy. Or maybe the dizziness was from the desire that throbbed through her, that made her press her body close to Ben. Close. Closer. *Not close enough.*

Did that urgent whimper come from her as Ben teased her taut nipples with his tongue? As he stroked her belly and below until she bucked against his hand with need? She gasped for breath as ripples of pleasure pulsed everywhere he touched. Revelled in the intensity of the intimacy they were sharing.

This was further than they'd gone the last time they'd been on this beach together. Now she wanted more. Much more. He was as ready for her as she was for him. She shifted her hips to accommodate him, to welcome him—at last.

Then she stilled at the same time as he did. Spoke at the same time as he did.

'Protection.'

'Birth control.'

He groaned, pressed a hard, urgent kiss against her mouth, then swung himself off the bed.

Sandy felt bereft of his warmth and presence. The bed seemed very big and empty without him. *Hurry, hurry, hurry back!* She wriggled on the quilt in an ecstasy of anticipation, pressed her thighs together hard. Twelve years she'd waited, and she didn't want to wait a second longer.

But she contained her impatience enough to watch in sensual appreciation as Ben, buck naked, strode without a trace of self-consciousness towards the tall dresser at the other side of the bed. He was magnificent, her surf god, in just his skin. Broad shoulders tapering to the tight defined muscles of his back; firm, strong buttocks, pale against the tan of the rest of him; long, muscular legs. A wave of pure longing for him swept through her and she gripped her hands tight by her sides.

He reached the dresser, pulled out the top drawer. *Yes! Get the protection and get back here. Pronto!*

But he hesitated—that taut, magnificent body was suddenly very still. Then he reached for a small framed photo that stood on the top of the dresser. It was too far away for Sandy to make out the details, just that there was a woman. Ben picked it up and slid it into the drawer, face downwards.

Sandy caught her breath.

Jodi. The photo must be of Jodi.

Ben didn't want her to see it. Didn't want Jodi seeing her naked on his bed.

And that was okay. Of course it was.

She had absolutely no reason to be upset by his action. He'd told her his late wife had loved him so unselfishly that she didn't want him to be alone. Sandy couldn't allow herself even a twinge of jealousy that Jodi had been the perfect wife.

But the desire that had been simmering though her suddenly went right off the boil. Despite the warmth of the day, she shivered. She pulled herself up on her elbows, looked around for something to cover her nakedness. She found his shirt, clutched it against her. It was still warm from his body heat.

Ben's gaze caught hers in a long, silent connection. Sandy's throat tightened. He knew she'd seen. But he didn't say anything. She knew he wouldn't. Knew she couldn't ask—in spite of his earlier frankness.

She realised with a painful stab of recognition that

Ben had gone so far away, in such a different direction from the youth they'd shared, that she didn't know him at all any more. For all they'd shared over the last twenty-four hours, today's Ben had been forged by loss and grief beyond her comprehension.

She'd loved Ben back then, with the fierce intensity of first love. But now? How could she love him when she didn't know him any more? Wasn't this just physical attraction she was feeling? She had never had sex without love. The fact was, though, she was the one who had encouraged this encounter. How could she back down now?

And yet his look of excited yet respectful anticipation made her swell with emotion. Did she love him again already? Was that what the heart-flipping thing was all about? Had her heart just taken up where it had left off twelve years ago? What if these four days were all she would ever have of him?

Desire warmed her again. She wanted him. She would take the chance.

She smiled as Ben impatiently pulled open the drawer. But the smile froze as he continued to dig through the contents. He swore. Slammed the door shut. Looked through another drawer. Then another. He threw out his hands in a gesture to indicate emptiness.

'None. No protection. You got any?' His voice was a burr of frustration and anger and something that could have been despair.

'No. I…uh…don't carry it with me.'

She'd had no use for protection for a long time. Seemed as if Ben was in the same boat.

He strode back and sat on the bed next to her. He smoothed back a lock of hair that had drifted across her cheek in a caress that was both gentle and sensual.

'I want you so much. But I won't risk getting you pregnant.'

An unplanned pregnancy wasn't on her agenda either. No way would she suggest taking that risk, much as she yearned for him. 'I'm not on the pill. S...sorry.'

'Why should you apologise?' He groaned. 'I should have—'

'Could we...could we go buy some?' As soon as the words were out of her mouth she knew that was a ridiculous idea. Ben acknowledged it with a grim smile. No doubt some busybody citizen of Dolphin Bay would be behind the counter at the pharmacy and only too eager to broadcast the news that Ben and his old girlfriend were in need of contraceptives.

'Okay...bad idea.' She didn't know what else she could say.

Ben's handsome face was contorted with frustration, his voice underscored with anguish. 'Sandy. You have to know I won't be a father again. Won't have another child. Not after what happened to my little boy. Can't risk that loss...that pain.'

Oh, Ben. Her heart felt as if it was tearing in sorrow for him, for the losses she couldn't even begin to imagine.

'I...I understand,' she stuttered. But did she? Could she ever comprehend the agony he felt at losing his child? 'D...do you want to talk about it?'

He shifted his body further from her. But more than a physical distance loomed between them. He took a deep, shuddering breath.

'You have a right to know why I feel this way.'

'Of course,' she murmured.

'When my mother knew Liam was on the way she told me that I wouldn't know what love was until I held my first child in my arms. I scoffed at her. I thought I knew what it was to love.'

'Lizzie said something similar after Amy was born.'

Ben swallowed hard. It must be agony for him to relive his memories.

'A father's love—it was so unexpected. So overwhelming. My mother was right. I would have done anything for my son.'

'Of course you would have,' she murmured, feeling helpless. She didn't know what to say—a thirty-year-old single whose only experience of loving a child was her niece.

'Changing nappies. Getting up at all hours of the night the minute I heard a whimper. Rocking him in my arms for hours to soothe him when he was teething. I did all that. But...but I couldn't save his life.'

Survivor's guilt. Post-traumatic stress. Labels she

thought might apply—but what did she know about how to help him?

'Ben, you're carrying a big burden. Did you have counselling to help you come to terms with your loss?'

As soon as the question left her mouth she knew it was a mistake. Ben so obviously *hadn't* come to terms with it.

His eyes were as bleak as a storm-tossed sea. 'I had counselling. But nothing can change the fact I couldn't save my baby son. End of story. On the day I buried him I vowed I would never have another child.'

'Because…because you think you don't deserve another child?'

'That too. But I couldn't bear the agony of loss again.'

She knew it wasn't the time to say that new life could bring new hope. That there was the possibility of loss any time you put your heart on the line. But how could she possibly understand what he'd gone through? Could she blame him for never wanting to risk finding himself in that unimaginably dark place again?

'Ben, I'm so sad for you.' She took his scarred, damaged hand in hers and squeezed it, wanting him to know how much she felt for him but was unable to express. He put his arms around her and pulled her tight. She nestled her face just below his shoulder, against the warm, solid muscle of his chest.

But she was sad for herself, too.

She thought back to her birthday goals. *Get married and have lots of kids. Three kids—two girls and a boy.*

It was as if Ben had read her mind. 'Remember how we used to talk about having kids? When were barely more than kids ourselves?'

'Yes,' she said. She swallowed hard against the lump of disappointment that threatened to choke her. She'd always seen being a mother in her future. Had never contemplated any other option.

He pulled back from her and she was forced to meet his gaze.

'So me not wanting kids could be a deal-breaker?'

She had to clear her throat before she answered, trying not to let him guess how shaken she was. 'Perhaps. For something long-term. But we're only talking four days, aren't we? It doesn't matter for... for a fling.'

'I guess not. But I wanted to make sure you knew where I stood.'

At the age of thirty she couldn't afford to waste time on any relationship—no matter how brief—that didn't have the possibility of children. Knowing that parenthood wasn't an option for Ben should make her pack up and leave Dolphin Bay right now. But she didn't have to think further than four days—and nothing could stop her from having this time with Ben. Come what may.

'I'm sorry, Sandy,' said Ben. 'This wasn't the way I thought things would pan out today.'

'It doesn't matter. I...I've lost the mood,' she confessed.

Suddenly she felt self-conscious being naked. With a murmur about being cold she disengaged herself from his arms. Fumbled around on the bed and found her dress. Pulled it over her head without bothering about wasting minutes with her bra. Wiggled into her panties. Found his clothes and handed them to him.

She felt very alone when he turned his back to her and dressed in awkward silence.

She sat on the edge of the bed and wondered how everything could have gone so wrong. 'Sunny Sandy', Ben had used to call her. But it was hard to see the glass-half-full side of finding out that he didn't ever want to have another child. And then there was that photo. How ready was he *really* to move on to another woman?

Ben wanted to pound the wall with his fists to vent his frustration and anger. He wanted to swear and curse. To fight his way through raging surf might help, too.

But he could do none of that. Sandy looked so woebegone sitting there, biting on her lip, her arms crossed defensively across her beautiful breasts. He had to control himself. Do anything in his power to reignite her smile.

His revelation that he didn't want more children had knocked the sunshine out of her. He appreciated how kind she'd been, how understanding, but dismay had shown on her face. But he'd had to put his cards on the table about a future with no children. He couldn't mislead her on such an important issue. Not that they were talking beyond these four days.

He reached out, took both her hands and pulled her to her feet.

'Sandy, I'm sorry—' he started.

'Don't say it again,' she said with a tremulous smile, and put her finger to his mouth. 'I'm sure we'll laugh about it one day.'

He snorted his disbelief. He would never see the humour in what had happened. Or had not happened.

'So what now?' she asked. 'Do I go back to the bookshop?'

He tightened his grip on her hands. 'No way. It's shut for the day. You're staying with me. We'll have lunch, then tonight I want to take you to a dinner dance.'

Her eyebrows rose. 'A dinner dance? In Dolphin Bay?'

She was such a city girl. She had no idea of how much the town had grown. How big his role as a business leader had become.

'The Chamber of Commerce annual awards night is being held at the hotel. As president, I'm presenting the awards. I'd like you to come.'

'As…as your date?'

'As my date.'

Her smile lit the golden sparks in her eyes in the way he remembered. 'I'd like that. This could be fun.'

'The speeches? Not so much. But there'll be a band and dancing afterwards.'

'Do you remember—?' she started.

'The dance?'

'I couldn't believe it when you asked me to dance with you.'

'I wasn't sure you'd say yes. You were the most beautiful girl there.'

She leaned up and kissed him on the mouth. 'Thank you for saying that.'

'You'll be the most beautiful girl there tonight.'

That earned him another kiss.

'Will I know anyone?'

'My parents. My brother, Jesse—he's back home for a couple days. Kate…'

Sandy's face tightened at the sound of Kate's name.

'Kate has a big mouth, but she also has a big heart,' he said.

'She can be confrontational.'

'Don't judge her too harshly. She means well.' He didn't want Sandy to feel alienated during her time in Dolphin Bay. That was one of the reasons he'd asked her to be his date for tonight, to go public with him. Encouraging a friendship with Kate was another.

'I'm sure she does. It's just that...'

'Yes?'

'Nothing,' she said, with an impish twist to her mouth.

He wasn't in the mood to argue with a female 'nothing'. 'C'mon. I'll make us some lunch.'

He kept her hand in his as he led her towards the kitchen.

'I didn't know you could cook,' she said.

She didn't know a lot about him. Some things she might never know. But his cooking prowess— or lack of it—was no secret.

'Basic guy-type stuff. Mostly I eat at the hotel. We could order room service if you want.'

'No. I like the idea of you cooking for me.'

She started to say something else but stopped herself. He wondered if her ex had ever cooked for her. He sounded like a selfish creep, so that was probably a no.

'What's on the menu, chef?' she asked.

'Take your pick. Toasted cheese sandwich or...' he paused for dramatic emphasis '...toasted cheese sandwich.'

'With ketchup? And Snickers for dessert? I have some in my handbag.'

'Done,' he said as he headed towards the fridge.

Without realising it, he started to whistle. He stopped himself. Why would he want to whistle when he was furious at himself for the disaster in the bedroom and fresh with the memories of his loss?

'That's a sound I haven't heard for a long time,' Sandy said as she settled herself on one of the bar stools that lined the kitchen counter.

'It's rusty from disuse,' he said.

'No, it isn't. I like it. Don't stop. Please.'

Her eyes were warm with concern and understanding. Her yellow dress flashed bright in the cool, neutral tones of the kitchen. Her brown hair glinted golden in the sunshine that filtered through the porthole windows. Sandy. Here in his home. The only woman he had brought here apart from his mother and the maids from the hotel who kept it clean.

He picked up the tune from where he had left off and started to whistle again.

CHAPTER ELEVEN

SANDY WAS ONLY too aware that every detail of her appearance would be scrutinised by the other guests at the Chamber of Commerce dinner dance. Every nuance of her interaction with Ben would be fuel for the gossipmongers of Dolphin Bay.

In one way it amused her. In another it scared her witless.

In spite of Ben's reassurances Kate's warning still disconcerted her. All the people who would be there tonight knew Ben. Had known Jodi. Had even—and her heart twisted painfully at the thought—known his baby son. She wouldn't be human if that didn't worry her.

She wished she and Ben could spend the entire time they had together alone in his boathouse home. Just him and her, and no one else to poke their noses into the one step forward and two steps back of their reunion. But it seemed it would be played out on the open stage of Ben's tight-knit community.

Thank heaven she'd packed a take-her-anywhere outfit for Melbourne. She checked her image in the mirror of her hotel room with a mega-critical eye. Dress? Red, strapless, short but not too short. Jewellery? A simple yet striking gold pendant and a blatantly fake ruby-studded gold cuff from one of her fashion accessory clients. Shoes? Red, sparkling, towering heels. She thought she would pass muster.

The look in Ben's eyes when he came to her room to pick her up told her she'd got it right.

For a moment he stood speechless—a fact that pleased her inordinately. He cleared his throat. 'You look amazing,' he said.

Amazing was too inadequate a word to describe how Ben looked in a tuxedo. The immaculately tailored black suit emphasised his height and the breadth of his shoulders, and set off the brilliant blue of his eyes. There was little trace of the teen surfer in the urbane adult who stood before her in the doorway to her room, but she didn't mourn that. The crinkles around his eyes when he smiled, the cropped darker hair, only added to his appeal. It struck her that if she met the grown-up Ben now, for the first time, as a total stranger, she'd be wildly attracted to him.

For a moment she was tempted to wind her arms around his neck and lure him into her room with whispered words of seduction. She thought of the birth control she had discovered tucked into a corner of her suitcase, accompanied by a saucy note from her sister, Lizzie: *In case you get lucky in Melbourne.*

But Ben had official duties to perform. She couldn't make him late.

'You look amazing yourself,' she said. She narrowed her eyes in a mock-appraising way. 'Kinda like a surf god crossed with a tycoon god.'

He rolled his eyes at her words but smiled. 'If you say so.'

Her stratospheric heels brought her to kissing distance from his face. She kissed him lightly on the cheek, but he moved his face so her lips connected with his mouth. She nearly swooned at the rush of desire that hit her. As she felt his tongue slip familiarly into her mouth she calculated how much time they had before they were due at the dinner dance. Ten minutes. Not enough time for what she needed from Ben if things were going to get physical again.

Besides, she wasn't so sure that was the way to go when their time together was so short. She didn't want to leave Dolphin Bay with a pulverised heart.

With a deep sigh of regret, she pulled away.

'C'mon, haven't you got awards to present?' she said.

She slipped her arm through his and they headed towards the elevator.

The first person Sandy saw when she walked with Ben into the hotel conference room where the dinner dance was being held was his mother. She clutched Ben's arm, shocked at the feeling of being cast back in time.

Maura Morgan had been wearing jeans and a T-shirt the last time she'd seen her; now she was wearing an elegant brocade dress. She was handsome, rather than beautiful, and she'd hardly changed in the intervening years. Her hair held a few more strands of grey, her figure was a tad more generous, but her smile was the same warm, welcoming smile that had made Sandy's stay at the guesthouse all those years ago so happy. And her voice still held that hint of a lyrical Irish accent that was a legacy of her girlhood in Dublin.

'Eh, Sandy, it's grand to see you. Who would have thought we'd see you here after all these years?' The older woman swept her into a warm hug.

'It's wonderful to see you again.' It was all Sandy could think of to say. But she meant every word. That summer, so long ago, there had been a wire of tension between her parents that at times had come close to snapping. Maura had been kind to her, and covered for her with her father when she'd snuck out to meet Ben.

Maura stepped back, with her hands still on Sandy's shoulders. 'Look at you, all grown up and even lovelier than when you were a girl—and friends with Ben again.' Her face stilled. 'Fate works in amazing ways.'

'It sure does,' Sandy agreed, reluctant to talk more deeply with Ben's mother. Not wanting to bring up the tragedies that had occurred since her last visit. She didn't know what Ben had told Maura about her reasons for staying in Dolphin Bay. The reignited feelings between her and Ben were so fragile—still just little sparks—she wanted to hug them close.

Maura released her. 'Your mum and dad…?'

Sandy shrugged. 'Divorced.'

Maura shook her head slowly. 'Why does that not surprise me? And your sister?'

'Lizzie's still my best friend. She has a little girl, Amy, who's five years old and a real cutie.'

As soon as she mentioned Amy, Sandy wished she hadn't. Ben's son Liam had been Maura's only grandchild. But Maura's smile didn't dim. 'It's lovely to hear that,' she said. 'And do you—?'

Ben interrupted. 'Mum, I've sat you and Dad at my table so you'll get a chance to talk to Sandy during the evening.

Maura laughed. 'So quit the interrogation? I hadn't yet asked Sandy if she has room in her heart for a homeless puppy.'

Ben groaned, but Sandy could hear the smile in his protest.

'A puppy? I'd love one,' she said without hesitation. 'That is if…' Her voice trailed away. *Get dog of own once settled in Melbourne.* Could she really commit to a dog when her future had become so uncertain? Until she knew exactly how she felt about Ben at the end of the four days?

Maura patted her hand. 'I won't hold you to the puppy until we've talked some more.'

The genuine warmth in her voice did a lot to reassure Sandy that Maura did not appear to have any objection to her reunion with Ben.

She felt she could face the rest of the evening with a degree less dread.

Sandy outshone any other woman in the room, Ben thought as he watched her charm the bank manager and his wife. It wasn't just the red dress, or the way the light caught her glittery shoes just like that darn fairy dust. It had more to do with the vivacity of her smile, the way her eyes gleamed with genuine interest at the details of the couple's daughter's high school results. He knew she was nervous, but no one would guess it.

It was a big, public step to bring her tonight—and he was glad he'd made it. It felt good to have her by his side. Instead of ill-disguised sorrow or embarrassed pity, he saw approval in the eyes of his family and friends. It was a big step forward.

But for the first time since he'd been elected president of the chamber Ben resented his duties. He didn't want to make polite chit-chat with the guests. He didn't want to get up there on stage and make a speech about the business community's achievements. Or announce the awards. He wanted to spend every second of the time he had left with Sandy— alone with her. They had less than four days—three days now—of catching up to do. If that included being behind closed doors, slowly divesting Sandy of that red dress and making love to her all night long, that was good too.

'We must catch up for coffee some time,' the banker's wife gushed in farewell to Sandy as Ben took Sandy's elbow to steer her away towards his table. He wanted her seated and introduced to everyone else at the table before he had to take his place on stage for the awards presentation.

'I'd like that,' Sandy called over her shoulder to the banker's wife as Ben led her away.

'Would you?' he asked in an undertone.

'Of course. She seems like a nice lady. But not any time soon.' She edged closer so she could murmur into his ear. 'We've only got a few days together. I want to spend every second of my spare time with you.'

'I'll hold you to that,' he said.

It felt unexpectedly good, being part of a couple again—even if only temporarily. He'd been on his own for so long. Maybe too long. But his guilt and regret still gnawed at him, punishing him, stopping him from getting close to anyone.

And now Sandy was back with him in Dolphin Bay.

The president's table was at the front of the room. His parents were already seated around it, along with Kate, his brother, Jesse, and two of the awards finalists—both women.

If his father remembered how disparaging he had been all those years ago about the sincerity of a city girl's feelings towards his son, he didn't show it. In his gruff way he made Sandy welcome.

Jesse couldn't hide the admiration in his eyes as he rose from his seat to greet Sandy. 'I would have recognised you straight away,' his brother said as he kissed her on the cheek.

Ben introduced Sandy to the awards finalists, then settled her into the seat between him and Kate. 'I have to finalise the order of proceedings. I'll be back in five minutes—in time for the appetiser,' he said.

He wanted to kiss Sandy. Claim her as more than a friend in front of all eyes. But it wasn't the right time. Instead, he brushed his hand over her bare shoulder in parting before he headed backstage. Only Kate's big grin made him realise the simple gesture was more a sign of possession than a friendly kiss on Sandy's cheek would ever have been.

Sandy heaved a quiet sigh of relief as she sank into her chair. The worst of the ordeal was behind her. From the moment she'd entered the room she'd been aware of the undercurrent of interest in her presence beside Ben. Her mouth ached from smiling. From formulating answers in reply to questions about how long she intended to be in town. Even though Ben had smoothed the way, she felt she was being judged on every word she spoke. She reached gratefully for her glass of white wine.

Ben's empty seat was to her left, between her and Kate. Tall, dark-haired Jesse—every bit as handsome as in her memories of him—sat on the other side of her, engaged in conversation with his mother.

Kate sidled close enough to whisper to Sandy. 'Note that Ben didn't sit me next to Jesse. Probably worried I'd fling myself on his brother, wrestle him to the ground and have my way with him under the table.'

Sandy nearly choked on her drink. 'Really?'

'Nah. Just kidding. I actually asked him not to put me near Jesse.' Kate's green eyes clouded. 'It's hard to make small-talk with the guy I've wanted all my life when he sees me as more sister than woman.'

'Can't he see how gorgeous you are?' Sandy asked. In an emerald silk dress that clung to her curves and flattered the auburn of her hair, Kate looked anything but the girl next door.

Kate pulled a self-deprecating face. 'Thanks. But it doesn't matter what I wear. To Jesse I'll always just be good old Kate, his childhood pal.'

'You never dated him?'

'We kissed when I was thirteen and he was fourteen. I never stopped wanting him after that.'

'And Jesse?'

Kate shrugged. 'He was a shy kid, and I guess I was a convenient experiment. It never happened again. Though I must have relived it a million times.'

'He certainly doesn't look shy now.'

Jesse's full attention was beamed on the attractive blonde award finalist.

'Yep. He's quite the man of the world these days,

and quite the flirt.' Kate kept her gaze on Jesse for a moment too long before returning it to Sandy.

Sandy's heart went out to Kate. 'That must be so tough for you. Ben told me Jesse's only visiting for a few days.'

'Yes. Jesse leads a construction team that builds low-cost housing in areas that have been destroyed by natural disasters. Think India, Africa, New Orleans. He only ever comes here between assignments.'

Sandy glanced again at Jesse. 'Good looks *and* a kind heart. No wonder you're hooked on him.'

'Kind hearts run in the Morgan family—as I think you well know.'

Was Kate about to give her another lecture about Ben? If so, she wasn't in the mood to hear it. 'Kate, I—'

Kate laughed and threw her hands up in a gesture of self-defence. 'I'm staying right out of the you-and-Ben thing. I've been warned.'

'Warned? By Ben?'

'Of course by Ben. You're important to him. Ben protects the people he cares about.'

Sandy loved the feeling Kate's words gave her. But, again, she sensed she might be getting out of her depth. Three more days in Dolphin Bay. That was all she was talking about after this evening. Deep in her heart, though, she knew there was a chance it could end up as so much more than that. She didn't know whether to be excited or terrified at the prospect.

After the starter course Ben took his place on stage. To Sandy, he looked imposing and every inch the powerful executive as he took the microphone to give a brief review of the year's past business activities. From the applause and occasional catcall from the audience it was apparent Ben was still very much the town's favourite son.

As he made a particularly pertinent point about the growth in revenue tourism had brought to Dolphin Bay Sandy thought she would burst with pride at his achievements, and at the way he had overcome such tragedy to get to this place. She wanted to get up from her seat and cheer. She caught his mother Maura's eye and saw the same pride and joy reflected in her face.

Maura acknowledged the thread of emotion that united them with a smile and a brief nod, before turning back to face the stage and applaud the end of Ben's speech.

Sandy smiled back—a wobbly, not very successful smile. *Maura knew.* She bit her lip and shredded the edge of her dolphin-printed serviette without really realising she was doing so.

Could she kid herself any further that all she wanted from Ben was a fling? Could she deny that if she didn't protect her heart she might fall right back in love? And then where would she be, if Ben decided four days of her was enough?

CHAPTER TWELVE

BUT SANDY'S HEART was singing as she danced with Ben. He danced as he'd danced with her that first time twelve years ago, and it seemed as if the years in between had never happened. Although they kept a respectable distance apart their bodies were in tune, hips swaying in unison with each other, feet moving to the same beat.

Most of the people in the room had also got up to dance once the formalities of the evening were done, but Sandy was scarcely aware of them. She couldn't keep her eyes off Ben or stop herself from 'accidentally' touching him at any opportunity— shoulders brushing, hips bumping, her hand skimming his as they moved their bodies in time to the music of a surprisingly good local band. And, in spite of the other guests' ill-concealed interest in the fact they were dancing together, Ben did nothing to move away.

She longed to be alone with him. He had rhythm, he had energy, he had power in that big, well-built body—and she ached to have it all directed to *her*. Upstairs in her bedroom.

When the band changed to slow dancing music, she was done for. As Ben pulled her into his arms and fitted his body close to her she wound her arms around her neck and sighed. 'How much longer do we have to endure this torture? If I have to explain to one more person than I'm just here for a few more days, I'll scream.'

'Same. The strain of all this focus on us is too much.'

'How much longer do we have to stay?'

He nuzzled into her neck, murmured low and husky. 'See those doors that open up to the balcony?'

She looked across the room. 'Yes.'

'We're going to dance our way over there and out on to the balcony, as if we're going for some fresh air—'

'Won't everyone think we've gone to make out?'

'Who cares?' He pulled her tighter. 'That way we don't have to announce our escape by exiting through the main doors.'

'What about your duties?'

'I'm done with duty.'

'So now you're all mine for the rest of the evening?' she murmured, with a provocative tilt of her head.

His eyes darkened to a deeper shade of blue and his grip tightened on her back. 'From the balcony we'll take the door to the empty conference room next door and then to the foyer.'

'And then?' Her voice caught in her throat.

'That's up to you.'

Her heart started doing the flippy thing so fast she felt dizzy. She pulled his head even closer to hers, brushed her lips across his cheek. 'Let's go,' she murmured.

He steered her through the crowd, exchanging quick greetings with the people they brushed past, but not halting for a moment longer than necessary. Sandy nodded, smiled, made polite responses, held on to his hand and followed his lead.

They sidled along the balcony, then burst into the empty conference room next door, laughing like truant schoolkids. Ben shut the door behind him and braced it in mock defence with an exultant whoop of triumph.

Sandy felt high on the same exhilaration she'd felt as a teenager, when Ben and she had successfully snuck away from their parents. She opened her mouth to share that thought with him, but before she could form the words to congratulate him on their clever escape he kissed her.

His kiss was hard and hungry, free of doubt or second thoughts. She kissed him back, matching his ardour. Then broke the kiss.

She took a few deep breaths to steady her thoughts. 'Ben, I'm concerned we're moving too fast. What do you think?'

Ben glanced at his watch. 'This day is nearly over. That leaves us three days. I want you, Sandy. I've always wanted you.'

'But what if we regret it? What if you—?' She was so aware of how big a deal it was for him to be with her. And the heartbreak she risked by falling for him again. She feared once she made love with him she would never want to leave him.

'I'll regret it more if we don't take this chance to be together. On our terms. No one else's.'

'Me too,' she said. No matter what happened after these three remaining days, she never wanted to feel again the regret that had haunted her all those years ago.

Please, let this be our time at last.

'My room or yours?' she said, putting up her face to be kissed again.

Ben couldn't bear to let go of Sandy even for a second. Still kissing her, he walked her through the door, out of the conference room and into the corridor. Still kissing her, he punched the elevator's 'up' button.

As soon as the doors closed behind them he nudged her up against the wall and captured her wrists above her head with one of his so much bigger hands. The walls were mirrored and everywhere he looked he saw Sandy in that sexy red dress, her hair tousled, her face flushed, her lips swollen from his kisses. Beautiful Sandy, who had brought hope back into his life.

The raising of her arms brought her breasts high out of her strapless dress to tease him. In the confines of the elevator the warm vanilla female scent of her acted like a mainline hit of aphrodisiac. He could make love to her there and then.

But, as it always had been with Sandy, this was about so much more than sex. This step they were about to take was as much about intimacy and trust and a possible move towards a future beyond the next three days. The responsibility was awesome.

It was up to him to make it memorable. He'd waited so long for her and he wanted their first time to be slow and thorough, not a heated rush that might leave her behind.

He trailed kisses down her throat to the swell of her breasts. She gasped and he tightened his grip on her hands. She started to say something but he kissed her silent. Then the elevator reached her floor.

Still kissing her, he guided Sandy out of the elevator and towards her room. He fished his master keycard out of his pocket, used it, then shouldered the door open. They stumbled into the room and he kicked the door shut behind them.

Sandy had imagined a sensual, take-their-time progression through the bases for her first-time lovemaking with Ben. But she couldn't wait for all that. It felt as if the entire day had been one long foreplay session. Every sense was clamouring for Ben. *Now.* Her legs were so shaky she could hardly stand.

She pulled away from the kiss, reached up and cradled his chin in her hands, thrilled at the passion and want in his eyes that echoed hers. Her breathing was so hard she had to gulp in air so her voice would make sense.

'Ben. Stop.'

Immediately, gentleman that he was, he made to pull away from her. Urgently she stilled him.

'Not stop. I mean go. Heck, that's not what I mean. I mean stop delaying. I swear, Ben, I can't wait any longer.' She whimpered. Yes, she whimpered—something she'd never thought she'd do for a man. 'Please.'

His eyes gleamed at the green light she'd given him. 'If you knew how difficult it's been to hold back…' he groaned.

'Oh, I have a good idea what it's been like,' she said, her heart pounding, her spirit exulting. 'I feel like I've been waiting for this—for you—all my life.'

She kicked off her shiny shoes, not caring where they landed. Ben yanked down the zipper of her dress. She tugged at his tuxedo jacket and fumbled with the buttons on his shirt. Before she knew it she stood in just the scantiest red lace thong and Ben was in nothing at all—his body strong and powerful and aroused, his eyes ablaze with need for her.

Beautiful wasn't a word she'd usually use to describe a man. But all her copywriting skills deserted her as she sought to find another word.

He was her once-in-a-lifetime love and she knew, no matter what happened tomorrow or the day after or the day after that, that tonight she would be irrevocably changed. As she took a step towards him she froze, overwhelmed—even a little frightened—of what this night might unleash. Then desire for this man took over again. Desire first ignited twelve long years ago. Desire thwarted. Desire reignited. Desire aching to be fulfilled.

Ben swept her into his arms and walked her towards the bed. Soon she could think of nothing but him and the urgent rhythm of the intimate dance they shared.

Ben didn't know what time it was when he woke up. There was just enough moonlight filtering through the gaps in the curtains for him to watch Sandy as she slept. He leaned on his elbow and took in her beauty.

She lay sprawled on her back, her right arm crooked above her head, the sheet tucked around her waist. Her hair was all mussed on the pillow. He was getting used to seeing it short, though he wished it was still long. In repose, her face had lost the tension that haunted her eyes. A smile danced at the corners of her mouth. She didn't look much older than the girl he'd thought he'd never see again.

It didn't seem real that she was here beside him.

Magic? Coincidence? Fate? Whatever—being with Sandy made him realise he had been living a stunted half-life that might ultimately have destroyed him.

How could he let her go in three days' time?

But if he asked Sandy to stay he had to be sure it would be to stay for ever.

With just one finger he traced the line of her cheekbones, her nose, her mouth.

She stirred, as he'd hoped she would. Her eyelids fluttered open and her gaze focused on him. His heart leapt as recognition dawned in her eyes. She smiled the slow, contented smile of a satisfied woman and stretched languorously.

'Fancy waking up to you in my bed,' she murmured. She took his hand and kissed first each finger in turn and then his palm with featherlight touches over the scars he hated so much. She placed his hand on her breast and covered it with her own.

'You were *so* worth waiting twelve years for,' she whispered.

'Yes.' He couldn't find any more words. Just kissed her on her forehead, on her nose, finally on her mouth.

Want for her stirred again. He circled her nipple with his thumb and felt it harden. She moaned that sweet moan of pleasure. She returned his kiss. Softly. Tenderly. Then she turned her body to his.

Afterwards she lay snuggled into him, her head nestled on his chest, their legs entwined. The sweet vanilla scent of her filled his senses. He held her to him as tightly as he could without hurting her. He didn't want to let her go.

Did she feel the same way about what had just happened—a connection that had been so much more than physical?

Did she know she had ripped down a huge part of the barricade that had protected him against feeling anything for anyone?

Hoarsely, he whispered her name.

The tenor of her breathing changed and he realised she was falling back to sleep. Had she heard him?

'Ben…' she murmured as her voice trailed away.

As Sandy drifted back into sleep, satiated not just with sexual satisfaction but with joy, she realised a profound truth: she'd never got it right with anyone but Ben. Not just the physical—which had been indescribably wonderful—but the whole deal.

Right back when she was eighteen she'd thought she'd found the man for her—but those close to her, those who had thought they knew what was best for her, had dissuaded her.

She tightened her grip on his hand and smiled.

Her heart had got it right the first time.

CHAPTER THIRTEEN

'So, is the sex with my nephew good?'

Sandy nearly fell off the chair near Aunt Ida's hospital bed, too flummoxed even to think about a reply.

Ida laughed. 'Not a question you expect a little old lady to ask?'

'Uh…not really,' Sandy managed to splutter as hot colour flooded her cheeks. She'd come to talk about the Bay Books business, not her private life with Ben.

Ida shifted her shoulders and resettled herself on the pillows, a flash of pain tightening her face. Sandy ached to help her, but Ben's great-aunt was fiercely independent.

'You don't actually have to answer me,' said Ida. 'But great sex is so important to a healthy relationship. If you don't have those fireworks now, forget having a happy future together.'

Sandy realised she had blushed more times since she'd been back in Dolphin Bay than she had in her entire life.

'I… Uh… We…' How the heck did Ida know what had happened with Ben last night? How did she know there'd been fireworks aplenty?

Ida chuckled. 'I'll take that as a yes, then. Any fool can see the chemistry between you two. Good. No matter what the world dishes up to you, you'll always have that wonderful intimacy to keep your love strong. It was like that for me and Mike.'

'Oh?' Sandy literally did not know where to look. To talk about sex with someone of her grandmother's age was a new and unnerving experience.

'I suppose you know about my scandalous past?'

'I heard that you—'

'But I guess you don't want to hear about that.'

The expression in Ida's eyes made it clear that Ida wanted very much to tell her story. And Sandy was curious to hear it. There hadn't been much talking about relationships in her family's strait-laced household. No wonder she'd been so naïve at the age of eighteen, when she'd met Ben.

Sandy settled herself back in her chair. 'Did you really run away with a sailor, like Ben says?'

'Indeed I did. Mike was sailing up the coast. We clicked instantly. I went back to his boat with him and—'

Sandy found herself gripping the fabric of her skirt where it bunched over her knees. She wanted to hear the story but she didn't—she *really* didn't—want to hear the intimate details.

'I never left. I quit my job. Threw my hat in with Mike. We got married on an island in Fiji.'

One part of Sandy thought it romantic, another thought it foolhardy.

'Even though you hardly knew him?' *But how well did she actually know Ben? Enough to risk her heart the way she'd done last night?*

'I knew enough that I wanted to spend every waking and sleeping moment with him. I was thirty-five; he was five years older. We didn't have time to waste.'

Was that message aimed at her and Ben? The way she felt right now Sandy hated being parted from him even for a minute. But there were issues still unresolved.

'What about…what about children? Did you regret not having kids?'

'Not for a moment. We couldn't have had the life we had with kids. Mike was enough for me.'

Could Ben be enough for her? Right now her heart sang with the message that he was all she wanted. But what about in years to come? If things worked out with Ben, could she give up her dreams of a family?

Ida continued. 'And I don't have time to waste now. Once I'm over this injury I want to go back to the places I visited with Mike. It might be my last chance.'

Sandy put up a hand in protest. 'Surely not. You—'

'Still have years ahead of me? Who knows? But what I *do* know is I need to sell Bay Books—and I want you to buy it from me.'

Again, Sandy was too flabbergasted to reply to the old lady. Just made an incoherent gasp.

'You told me you want to run your own business,' said Ida. 'And I'm talking a good price for stock, fittings and goodwill.'

'Yes… But…'

But why not?

Candles came a poor second to books. And she already had so many ideas for improving Bay Books. Hadn't she thought, in the back of her mind, that if there were a chance she might stay in Dolphin Bay she would need to earn her living?

'Why the "but"?' Ida asked.

'The "but" is Ben,' said Sandy. 'We're not looking beyond these next few days right now. I have to take it slowly with him. I'm interested in your proposition. But I can't commit to anything until I know if there might be anything more with Ben.'

Ida's eyes were warm with understanding. 'I know what Ben's been through. I also know he needs to look to the future. I'm hoping it's with you.'

'Thank you,' said Sandy, touched by the older lady's faith in her.

'I'll keep my offer on the table. But I'll be selling—if not to you, to someone else.'

'Can we keep this between us?' Sandy asked. 'I'd

rather not mention it to Ben just yet. I don't want him to think I'm putting any pressure on him.'

'Of course,' said Ida.

Sandy felt guilty, putting a 'Back in One Hour' sign on the door of Bay Books—but meeting Ben for lunch was more important.

Ida's words echoed through her head. *She didn't have time to waste.*

She made her way to the boathouse to find the door open and Ben unpacking gourmet sandwiches from the hotel café and loading cold drinks into the refrigerator.

Again, he was whistling, and she smiled at the carefree sound. He hadn't realised she was there and she was struck by the domesticity of the moment. Did she want this with Ben? Everyday routine as well as heart-stopping passion? Much, much more than a few days together?

The answer was in his eyes when he looked up and saw she was there. *Yes. Yes. Yes.*

Yes to sharing everything.

Everything but the rearing of kids.

He put down the bottle he was holding, she dropped her handbag, and they met in the middle of the room. Ben held her close. She stood in his arms, exulting in the warm strength of him, the thudding of his heart, the way he smelled of the sea.

'I'm glad you're here,' he said.

'Me too,' was the only reply she could manage.

Her heart started a series of pirouettes—demanding its message be heard.

She loved him.

Emotion, overwhelming and powerful, surged through her. So did gratitude for whatever power had steered her back to him.

But could wounded, wary Ben love her back in the way she needed?

He kissed her—a brief, tender kiss of welcome—then pulled away.

'How did it go with Ida at the hospital?'

When she told him about Ida's questioning about their love-life he laughed, loud and uproariously.

'The old girl is outrageous,' he said, with more than a hint of pride. 'So what did you say to her?'

'I was so embarrassed I didn't know where to look.'

He pulled her close again. His voice was deep and husky and suggestive. 'What *would* you have told her?'

She twined her arms around his neck. 'I think you know last night was the most amazing experience of my life.' She had trouble keeping her voice steady. 'Why didn't I say yes all those years ago? Why, why, *why* didn't I fight harder for you?'

'Water under the bridge, remember?'

'Yes, but—'

'It mightn't have been such an amazing experience when I was nineteen.'

'Not true. You were the best kisser. Still are.'

'Always happy to oblige,' he said.

She smiled. 'Last night…the dinner dance…it was fun, wasn't it?'

'You were a big hit.'

'Was I? I'm still not quite sure how to handle the townfolk. In particular the way they compare me to Jodi.' *And I'm not sure how, if we have a future, I'll handle being second in your life.*

'You're still worrying about that?' He took her hand and led her to the bedroom. 'There's something I want to show you.'

'And I'm quite happy to see it,' she quipped. 'We can eat lunch afterwards.'

He laughed. 'That's not what I meant. But we can do that too.'

He went to the dresser. He opened the top drawer and pulled out the framed photo he had put there yesterday—the yesterday that seemed a hundred years ago. She braced herself, not at all sure she could cope with seeing Jodi and Ben together in happy times. She prayed the baby wouldn't be in the photo. One day she would have to go there. But not now. Not when this was all too raw and new.

Ben held the photo so she couldn't see what it was. 'It concerned me when you said you were worried about coming second with me. About being in the shadow of the memory of another woman. It's ironic that Jodi felt the same way about you.'

Sandy frowned. 'What do you mean?'

He handed her the photo. Astounded, she looked

from it to him and back again. 'But it's of me. Of you. Of *us*.'

The simple wooden frame held a faded snap of her very young self and Ben with their arms around each other. She—super-slim—was wearing a tiny pink floral-patterned bikini; her hair was wet and tangled with salt and fell almost to her waist. She was looking straight at the camera with a confident, happy smile. Ben's surfer hair was long and sunstreaked and he was wearing blue Hawaiian print board shorts. He wasn't looking at the camera but rather down at her, with an expression of pride and possession heartrendingly poignant on a teenager.

She had to clear her throat before she spoke. 'Where did you get this from?'

'From you. Don't you remember?'

Slowly the memory returned to her. 'Lizzie took this photo. We had to get the film developed at the chemist in those days. I bought the frame from the old general store. And I gave it to you to…to remember me by.' She'd had a copy, too. Had shoved it in the back of an old photo album that was heaven knew where now.

'Jodi found it at the bottom of a drawer in my room just before we got married. She brought it to me and said we needed to talk.'

'I…I thought you would have thrown it out.'

'She thought so too. She asked me was I still carrying a torch for you.'

'Wh…what did you say?'

'I said I'd cared for you once but was now totally committed to her.'

Sandy swallowed hard against a kick of that unwarranted jealousy. 'You…you were getting married. Wouldn't she *know* that?'

'We were getting married because she was pregnant with Liam.'

Sandy let out a gasp of surprise. 'I…I didn't know that.'

'Of course you didn't. But she was sensitive about it. Wanted me to reassure her that I wasn't marrying her just because I "had to".'

'Poor Jodi.' Her heart went out to the lovely girl who had cared so much for Ben, and she wished she had more than vague memories of her.

'So, you see, as far as Jodi was concerned you were the "third person", as you put it, in our marriage.'

'I…I don't really know what to say. If…if you were married I wouldn't come anywhere near you.'

'I know that. You know that. And I'm sure Jodi knew that. But no matter how much I reassured her that we would have got married anyway, just maybe not so soon, she had that little nagging doubt that she was my second choice.'

'And yet you…you didn't throw out the photo.' She was still holding the frame in her hands, her fingers tightly curled around the edge.

'No. I went to put it in the bin, to prove my point, but Jodi stopped me. Said it was unrealistic to expect we wouldn't each come into the marriage with a past. She just wanted to make sure you stayed in the past.'

'And here I am…in…in the future.'

'I hadn't thought about this photo in years. Then, after that morning on the beach with you and Hobo, I dug it out from a box in the storeroom at the hotel.'

'And put it on display?'

Ben took the photo frame from her hands and placed it back on top of the dresser. 'Where it will stay,' he said.

'So…so why did you hide it from me yesterday?'

'I thought you'd think it was strange that I'd kept it. It was too soon.'

'But it's not too soon now?'

'We've come a long way since yesterday.'

'Yes,' she said. She made a self-conscious effort to laugh. But it came out as something more strangled. 'Who knows where we'll get to in the next three days?'

It was a rhetorical question she wished she hadn't uttered as soon as she'd said it. But Ben just nodded.

He picked up the photo frame and then put it back down again. 'If you're okay with it, I'll keep it here.'

'Of course,' she said, speaking through a lump of emotion in her throat. 'And I don't expect you to keep photos of Jodi buried in a drawer while I'm around.'

But, please, no photos of Liam on display. No way could she deal with that while she was dealing with the thought that if it worked out with Ben she would see the demise of her dream of having her own kids.

'She was a big part of my life. I'm glad you don't want to deny that.'

'Of course I recognise that. Like…like she did about me.'

She looked again at the long-ago photo and wondered how Jodi had felt when she'd seen it. How sensible Jodi had been not to deny Ben his past. She had to do the same. But there was still that nagging doubt.

'I still can't help but wonder if I can compete with the memory of someone so important to you.'

He cupped her chin with his big scarred hands. 'As I said before, it's not a competition. You're so different. She was the safe harbour, calm waters. You're the breaking waves, the white-water excitement.'

'Both calm waters and breaking waves can be good,' she said, understanding what he meant and feeling a release from her fears. She hoped she, too, could at times become a safe harbour for him.

If she were to carry the wave analogy to its conclusion, Jason had been the dumper wave that had started off fast and exciting and then crashed her, choking and half drowning, onto the hard, gritty sand.

But what she felt for Ben defied all categorisation. He was both safe harbour and wild wave, and everything else she wanted, in one extraordinary man. And she longed to be everything to him.

But she couldn't tell him that. Not yet. Not until the three days were over.

'How long until you have to be back at the shop?' Ben asked.

'How long do we need?' she murmured as she slid her arms around his waist and kissed him.

CHAPTER FOURTEEN

SANDY TURNED THE 'Back in One Hour' sign—it had stretched to one and a half hours—so it read 'Open' and dashed into the shop. She spent a few minutes fixing her hair and make-up so the next contingent of too-interested ladies who came in wouldn't immediately guess how she'd spent her lunch hour. Wouldn't *that* make the Dolphin Bay grapevine hum…?

But customers were few—maybe she wasn't such a novelty any more. Or maybe, because it was such a hot day, people would rather be on the beach. She lifted her hair from her neck to cool it. It was warm in here today, despite her fiddling with the air-conditioning controls.

In the lull, after a lady had been seeking the latest celebrity chef cookbook and a man had wanted a history of the Dolphin Bay fishing fleet, she pulled out her fairy notebook. The glitter shimmered onto the countertop. It was time to revisit her thirtieth birthday resolutions.

She read them through again, with her Hotel Harbourside pen poised to make amendments.

1. Get as far away from Sydney as possible while remaining in realms of civilisation and within reach of a good latte.

Tick.
Dolphin Bay was four hours away from Sydney, and Ben's hotel café did excellent coffee. But her stay depended on a rekindled relationship of uncertain duration.

2. Find new job where can be own boss.

Tick.
The possibility of owning Bay Books exceeded the 'new job' expectations. She scribbled, *Add gift section to bookshop—enquire if can be sub-franchisee for candles.*

But, again, the possible job depended entirely on her relationship with Ben. She wouldn't hang around in Dolphin Bay if they kissed goodbye for good on Wednesday.

She hesitated when she came to resolution number three. As opposed to the flippy thing, her heart gave a painful lurch.

3. Find kind, interesting man with no hang-ups who loves me the way I am and who wants

*to get married and have three kids, two girls
and a boy.*

She'd found the guy—though he came with hang-
ups aplenty—and maybe he was the guy on whom
she'd subconsciously modelled the brief. But as for
the rest of it....

Could she be happy with just two out of three
resolutions fulfilled? How big a compromise was
she prepared to make?

Now her heart actually ached, and she had to
swallow down hard on a sigh. Children had always
been on the agenda for her—in fact she'd never
imagined a life that didn't include having babies.
Then her mother's oft-repeated words came to mind:
'*You can't have everything you want in life, Alexandra.*'

She put down her pen, then picked it up again.
Channelled 'Sunny Sandy'. Two out of three was
definitely a cup more than half full. Slowly, with a
wavering line of ink, she scored through the words
relating to kids, then wrote: *If stay in DB, ask Maura
about puppy.* She crossed out the word 'puppy' and
wrote *puppies.*

Unable to bear any further thoughts about shelv-
ing her dreams of children, she slammed the fairy
notebook shut.

As she did so the doorbell jangled. She looked
up to see a very small person manfully pushing the
door open.

'Amy! *Sweetpea!*'

Sandy flew around the counter and rushed to meet her niece, then looked up to see her sister, Lizzie, behind her. 'And Lizzie! I can't believe it.'

Sandy greeted Lizzie with a kiss, then swept Amy up into her arms and hugged her tight. Eyes closed at the bliss of having her precious niece so close, she inhaled her sweet little-girl scent of strawberry shampoo and fresh apple.

'I miss you, bub,' she said, kissing Amy's smooth, perfect cheek.

'Miss you too, Auntie Ex.'

Her niece was the only person who called her that—when she was tiny Amy hadn't been able to manage 'Alexandra' and it had morphed into 'Ex', a nickname that had stayed.

'But you're squashing me.'

'Oh, sorry—of course I am.' Sandy carefully put her niece down and smoothed the fabric of Amy's dress.

Amy looked around her with wide eyes. 'Where are the books for children?' she asked.

'They're right over here, sweetpea. Are your hands clean?'

Amy displayed a pair of perfectly clean little hands. 'Yes.'

'Then you can take books and look at them. There's a comfy purple beanbag in the corner.'

Amy settled herself with a picture book about a crocodile. Sandy had trouble keeping her eyes off her little niece. Had she grown in just the few days since they'd said goodbye in Sydney? Amy had been a special part of her life since she'd been born and she loved being an aunt. She'd looked forward to having a little girl just like her one day.

Her breath caught in her throat. *If she stayed with Ben no one would ever call her Mummy.*

'Nice place,' said Lizzie, looking around her. 'But what the heck are you doing here? You're meant to be on your way to Melbourne.'

'I could ask the same about you. Though it's such a nice surprise to see you.'

'Amy had a pupil-free day at school. I decided to shoot down here and see what my big sis was up to!'

'I texted you.'

'Just a few words to say you were spending some time in Dolphin Bay. Dolphin Bay! Why *this* end-of-nowhere dump? Though I have to say the place has smartened itself up. And Amy loves the dolphin rubbish bins.'

'I took the scenic route down the coast. It was lunchtime when I saw the turn-off, and—'

Lizzie put up her hand to halt her. 'I suspected it, but now I get it. This is about Ben Morgan, isn't it? What else would the attraction be here? And don't even *think* about lying, because you're blushing.'

'I have caught up with Ben. Yes.'

Lizzie took a step closer. 'You've done a lot more than "caught up" with Ben, haven't you?'

Sandy rolled her eyes skyward and laughed. Then

she filled her sister in on what had happened since she'd driven her Beetle down the main street of Dolphin Bay. Including Ida's offer to sell her Bay Books, but excluding Ben's decision not to have any more children.

'So, are you going to stay here with Ben?' Lizzie asked.

Sandy shrugged. 'We're testing the waters of what it might be like. But I feel the same way about him as I did back then.'

Lizzie stayed silent for a long moment before she spoke again. 'You're not just getting all sentimental about the past because of what happened with Jason?'

Sandy shook her head. 'Absolutely not. It's nothing to do with that. Just about me and Ben.'

Just mentioning their names together made her heart flip.

'I remember what it was like between you. Man, you were crazy about each other.'

Sandy clutched her sister's arm. Lizzie had to believe that what she'd rediscovered with Ben was the real deal. 'It's still there, Lizzie, that feeling between us. We took up where we left off. I'm so happy to have found him again. Even if these few days are all we have. And I don't give a toss about Jason.'

'I'm thrilled for you—truly I am. I always liked Ben. And I love this shop. It would be cool to own it. Way better than candles.' Lizzie shifted from foot to foot. 'But now I've brought up the J word I have to tell you something. You're going to hear it sooner or later, and I'd rather you heard it from me.'

Sandy frowned. 'Is it about the wedding?' She hadn't given it another thought.

'More about the bump under What's-Her-Name's wedding gown.'

Sandy had to hold on to the edge of the closest bookshelf. 'You mean—?'

'They're not admitting to it. But the wedding guests are betting there'll be a J-Junior coming along in about five months' time.'

Sandy felt the blood drain from her face. Not that she gave a flying fig for That-Jerk-Jason. But envy of his new bride shook her. Not envy of her having Jason's baby. The thought of anyone other than Ben touching her repulsed her. But envy because *she* would never be the one with a proudly displayed bump, would never bear Ben's child.

'Are you okay, Sandy?'

Sandy took a deep breath, felt the colour rush back into her face. 'Of course I'm okay. It's a bit of a shock, that's all.'

Lizzie hugged her. 'Maybe you'll be next, if you end up with Ben. You're thirty now—you won't want to leave it too long.'

'Of course not,' said Sandy, her voice trailing away.

Lizzie was just the first to say it. If, in some hypothetical future, she and Ben decided to stay together it would start. First it would be, *So when are you two tying the knot?* followed by, *Are you putting on weight or have you got something to tell us?*

Would she would be able to endure her friends' pregnancy excitement, birth stories, christenings, first-day-at-school sob-stories? All the while knowing she could never share them?

She understood Ben's stance against having another child. Was aware of the terrible place it came from. But she couldn't help but wonder if to start a relationship with Ben predicated on it being a relationship without children would mean a doomed relationship. It might be okay to start with, but as the years went by might she come to blame him? To resent him?

'You sure you're okay?' asked Lizzie. 'You look flushed.'

'Really, I'm fine.' Sandy fanned her face with both hands. 'It's hot. I suspect this rattly old air-conditioner is on its last legs.'

'You could put in a new one if you bought the business.'

'I guess…' she said, filled with sudden new doubt.

Holding Amy in her arms, hearing about Jason's bride's bump, had shaken her confidence in a long-term relationship with Ben that didn't include starting a family.

She changed the subject. 'What are you guys planning on doing? Can you stay tonight?'

'That depends on you. I promised Amy I'd take her to see the white lions at Mogo Zoo. Then we could come back here, have dinner with you and Ben, stay the night and go home tomorrow.'

'That would be amazing. Let's book you into Ben's gorgeous hotel.'

When had her thoughts changed from Hotel Hideous to 'Ben's gorgeous hotel'?

She didn't feel guilty about putting the 'Back in Ten Minutes' sign up on the bookshop door—Ida had quite a collection of signs, covering all contingencies. It was hot and stuffy inside Bay Books and she was beginning to feel claustrophobic.

And she wanted to see Ben again, to be reassured that loving him would be enough.

Ben was stunned to see Sandy coming towards Reception with a little girl. The child was clutching one of Bay Books' brown paper bags with one hand and holding on tight to Sandy's hand with the other. All the while she kept up a steady stream of childish chatter and Sandy looked down to reply, her face tender and her eyes warm with love.

That newly tuned engine of his heart spluttered and stalled at the sight. It looked natural and right to see Sandy hand in hand with a child. The little girl might be her daughter.

Anguish tore through him. Liam would have been around the same age if he'd lived. *He could not go there.* Getting past what would have been Liam's first birthday had seen him alone in his room with a bottle of bourbon. The other anniversaries had been only marginally better.

Sandy caught sight of him and greeted him with a big smile. Was he imagining that it didn't reach her eyes? He forced himself to smile back, to act as though the sight of her with a child had not affected him.

He pulled her into a big hug. His need to keep their relationship private from the gossiping eyes of Dolphin Bay was in the past. He'd been warmed and gratified by the good wishes he'd been given since the night of the Chamber of Commerce dance. He hadn't realised just how concerned his family and friends had been about him.

'This is my niece, Amy,' Sandy said. 'Amy, this is my friend Ben.'

Ben hunkered down to Amy's height. 'Hi, Amy. Welcome to Dolphin Bay.'

'I like dolphins,' Amy said. 'They smile. I like crocodiles too. I've got a new crocodile book.' She thrust the brown paper bag towards him.

'That's good,' Ben said awkwardly. He was out of practice with children. Hadn't been able to deal with them since he'd lost Liam.

Sandy rescued him from further stilted conversation. 'Do you remember my sister, Lizzie?' she asked, indicating the tall blonde woman who had joined them.

'Of course I remember you, Lizzie,' he said as he shook hands. Though, truth be told, back then he'd been so caught up with Sandy he'd scarcely noticed Lizzie, attractive though she was.

'Who would have thought I'd see you two together again after all these years?' said Lizzie.

'Yes,' he said.

He looked down at Sandy and she smiled up at him.

'Can we book Lizzie and Amy into a room with a water view?' she asked.

We. She'd said 'we'. And he wasn't freaked out by it as much as he'd thought he would be. In fact he kind of liked it.

He put his arm around her and held her close. She clutched onto him with a ferocity that both pleased and worried him. There was that shadow again around her eyes. *What gave?*

He booked Lizzie and Amy into the room adjoining Sandy's, talking over their protests when he told them that the room was on the house.

'Dinner tonight at the hotel?' he asked, including Lizzie and Amy in the invitation.

Sandy nodded. 'Yes, please—for all of us. Though it will have to be early because of Amy's bedtime.'

'I'm good with that.'

The sooner Lizzie and Amy were settled in their room, the sooner he could be alone with Sandy. Their time together was ticking down.

Lizzie glanced at her watch. 'We have to get to the zoo.' She took Amy's book and packed it in her bag. 'C'mon, Amy, quick-sticks.'

Amy indicated for Sandy to pick her up and Sandy obliged. She embraced Sandy in a fierce hug.

'I'll bring you a white lion, Auntie Ex,' she said.

Auntie Ex? Ben was about to ask for an explanation of the name when Amy leaned over from her position in Sandy's arms and put her arms up to be hugged by him.

'Bye-bye, Ben,' she said. 'Do you want a white lion, too?'

Ben froze. He hadn't held a child since he'd last held Liam. But Amy's little hands were resting on his shoulders, her face close to his. For a moment it was the three of them. A man. A woman. A child.

He panicked. Had to force himself not to shake. He looked to Sandy over the little girl's blonde head. Connected with her eyes, both sad and compassionate.

He cleared his throat and managed to pat the little girl gently on the back. 'A white lion would be great—thanks, Amy.'

'A girl one or a boy one?' Amy asked.

Ben choked out the words. 'A…a boy one, please.'

'Okay,' she said, and wiggled for Sandy to put her down.

Amy ran over to her mother.

'How are you going to get the white lions back here, Amy?' asked Sandy.

'In the back of the car, of course, silly,' Amy replied.

The adults laughed, which broke the tension. But

Ben was still shaken by the emotion that had over-taken him when he'd stood, frozen, in that group hug with Sandy and Amy. And he couldn't help but notice how Sandy's eyes never left her delight-ful little niece. There was more than being a doting aunt in her gaze.

'Okay, guys, I have to get back to the bookshop,' Sandy said. She hugged Amy and Lizzie. Then turned to him and hugged him. 'I'm going to stay back for a little while after I shut up shop and flick through Ida's files. I'll see you for dinner.'

He tightened his arms around her. Something was bothering her—and that bothered him. 'Don't be too long,' he said, wanting to urge her to stay.

Lizzie and Amy headed for their car. Ben watched Sandy as she walked through the door. Her steps were too slow, her head bowed. She seemed sud-denly alone, her orange dress a flash of colour in the monochrome decor of the reception area.

Was she thinking about how much she'd miss Lizzie and Amy if she settled in Dolphin Bay?

He suspected it was more than that.

Sandy had accepted his reasons for not wanting to risk having another child. But he'd seen raw longing in her eyes when she'd been with Amy.

When she was eighteen she'd chattered on that she wanted three kids. He'd thought two was enough—but he hadn't argued about wanting to be a parent. Fatherhood had been on his future agenda, too.

The ever-present pain knifed deeper. Being father

to Liam had been everything he'd wanted and more. He'd loved every minute of his son's babyhood.

He took in a deep, shuddering breath. By denying Sandy her chance to be a mother he could lose her. If not now, then later.

It might make her wave goodbye and leave for Melbourne on Wednesday, never to return to Dolphin Bay. Or, if she decided to stay with him, she might come to resent him. Blame him for the ache in her heart that only a baby could soothe.

Could he let that happen?

CHAPTER FIFTEEN

THE NEXT AFTERNOON Sandy trudged towards the hospital entrance. Fed up with the muggy atmosphere in Bay Books, and the rattling, useless air-conditioner, she'd shut up shop on the dot of five o'clock. To heck with going through more of Ida's files. She'd talk to Ida in person.

Whether or not she'd be able to have a sensible business conversation was debatable. She was too churned up with anxiety about the reality that a long-term relationship with Ben meant giving up her dream of having children. She tried summoning the techniques Ben had taught her to overcome her fear of monster waves but without any luck.

Her anxiety was like a dark shadow, diminishing the brilliance of her rediscovered love for Ben. Even memories of their heavenly lovemaking the night before, the joy of waking again in his arms, was not enough.

It felt like that long-ago summer day when she had been snorkelling with Ben at Big Ray Beach, out in the calm waters of the headland. It had been a perfect day, the sun shimmering through the water to the white sand beneath them, illuminating shoals of brightly coloured little fish darting in and out of the rocks. She and Ben had dived to follow some particularly cute orange and white clown fish.

Then suddenly everything had gone dark. Terrified, she'd gripped Ben's arm. He'd pointed upwards and she'd seen one of the big black manta rays that had given its name to the beach swim directly above them. She'd panicked, thinking she didn't have enough air to swim around it and up to the surface. But the ray had cruised along surprisingly quickly and she and Ben had been in sunshine again. They'd burst through to the top, spluttering and laughing and hugging each other.

Right now she felt the way she had when the light had been suddenly cut off.

She couldn't ignore Ben's stricken reaction when Amy had reached out to him yesterday. Her niece was discerning when it came to the adults she liked. She'd obviously picked Ben as a good guy and homed in like a heat-seeking missile. But all it had done was bring back painful memories for Ben.

If Sandy had held on to any remnant of hope that Ben might change his mind about having a child she'd lost it when she'd seen the fear and panic in his eyes.

And it hadn't got any better during dinner. She'd seen what an enormous effort it had been for Ben to take part in Amy's childish conversation. Amy, bless her, hadn't noticed. Her little niece had been too pleased she'd managed to get a toy girl white lion for her Auntie Ex and a boy one for Ben.

It must be so painful for Ben to endure—every child he encountered a reminder to him of what he had lost.

But it was painful for her, too, to know that Amy would be the only child she would ever have to love if she and Ben became a long-term couple.

Could she really do this? Put all her hopes of a family aside?

Would she be doomed to spend the next ten years or so hoping Ben might change his mind? Counting down the fertile years she had left? Becoming embittered and resentful?

She loved Ben; she didn't want to grow to hate him.

If she had any thought that her relationship with Ben might founder over the children issue should she think seriously of breaking it off now, to save them both future pain? Her heart shrivelled to a hard, painful knot at the thought of leaving him.

She couldn't mention her fears to Lizzie—now back home in Sydney. Lizzie would tell her to run, not walk, away from Dolphin Bay. Her sister had often said giving birth to Amy was the best thing that had ever happened to her. She wouldn't want Sandy to miss out on motherhood.

Ben's decision not to have more children really could be a deal-breaker. Tomorrow was Wednesday and their future beyond tonight had become the elephant in the room. No. Not just an elephant but a giant-sized woolly mammoth.

As she neared the big glass doors of the hospital entrance she knew she had to tell Ida to take her out of the Bay Books equation. She couldn't consider her offer while she had any doubt at all about staying in Dolphin Bay.

But almost as soon as she was inside the hospital doors she was waylaid by the bank manager's wife, a hospital administrator, who wanted to chat.

By the time she got to Ida's bedside it was to find Ben's aunt in a highly agitated state.

'Why haven't you answered your mobile? There's smoke pouring out of Bay Books. Ben's there, investigating.'

It was nothing Ben could put his finger on, but he could swear Sandy had distanced herself from him last night. Especially through that awkward dinner. At any time he'd expected outspoken Lizzie to demand to know what his intentions were towards Sandy. And Sandy's obvious deep love for Amy had made him question again the fairness of depriving her of her own children.

But tomorrow was Wednesday. He *had* to talk with Sandy about her expectations—and his—if they were to go beyond these four awesome days.

She wasn't picking up her mobile. Seeing her would be better. He headed to Bay Books.

Ben smelled the smoke before he saw it—pungent, acrid, burning the back of his throat. Sweat broke out on his forehead, dampened his shirt to his back. His legs felt like lead weights. Terror seized his gut.

Sandy. Was she in there?

He was plunged back into the nightmare of the guesthouse fire. The flames. The doorknob searing the flesh of his hands. His voice raw from screaming Jodi's name.

His heart thudded so hard it made him breathless. He forced his paralysed legs to run down the laneway at the side of the shop, around to the back entrance. Dark grey smoke billowed out through a broken pane in the back window.

The wooden carvings. The books. So much fuel for the fire. A potential inferno.

Sandy could be sprawled on the floor. Injured. Asphyxiated. He had to go in. Find her.

Save her.

He shrugged off his jacket, used it to cover his face, leaving only a slit for his eyes. He pushed in his key to the back door and shoved. The door gave. He plunged into the smoke.

'Sandy!' he screamed until his voice was hoarse.

No response.

Straight away he saw the source of the smoke. The old air-conditioning unit on the wall that Ida had refused to let him replace. Smouldering, distorted by heat, but as yet with no visible flames.

The smoke appeared to be contained in the small back area.

But no Sandy.

Heart in his mouth, he shouldered open the door that led through into the shop. No smoke or flames.

No Sandy there either.

All the old pain he'd thought he'd got under control gripped him so hard he doubled over. What if it had been a different story and Sandy had died? By opening up to Sandy he'd exposed himself again to the agony of loss.

He fought against the thought that made him wish Sandy had never driven so blithely back into Dolphin Bay. Making him question the safe half-life that had protected him for so long.

Like prison gates clanging shut, the old barriers against pain and loss and anguish slammed back into place. He felt numb, drained.

How could he have thought he could deal with loving another woman?

A high-pitched pop song ringtone rang out, startling him. It was so out of place in this place of near disaster. He grabbed Sandy's mobile phone from next to the register and shoved it in his pocket without answering it. Why the *hell* didn't she have it with her?

He headed back to the smouldering air-conditioning unit, grabbed the fire extinguisher canister from the nearby wall bracket and sprayed fire retardant all over it.

Then he staggered out into the car park behind the shop.

He coughed and spluttered and gulped in huge breaths of fresh air.

And then Sandy was there, her face anguished and wet with tears.

'Ben. Thank heaven. *Ben.*'

Sandy never wanted to experience again the torment of the last ten minutes. All sorts of hideous scenarios had played over and over in her head.

She scarcely remembered how she'd got from the hospital to Bay Books, her heart pounding with terror, to find horrible black smoke and Ben inside the shop.

But Ben was safe.

His face was drawn and stark and smeared with soot. His clothes were filthy and he stank of acrid smoke. But she didn't care. She flung herself into his arms. Pressed herself to his big, solid, blessedly alive body. Rejoiced in the pounding of his heart, the reassuring rise and fall of his chest as he gulped in clean air.

'You're okay…' That was all she could choke out.

He held her so tightly she thought he would bruise her ribs.

'It wasn't as bad as it looked. There's just smoke damage out the back. It didn't reach the books.'

He coughed. Dear heaven, had the smoke burned his throat?

Relief that he was alive morphed into anger that he'd put himself in such danger. She pulled back and pounded on his chest with her fists. 'Why did you go in there? Why take the risk? Ida must have insurance. All that wood, all that paper... If it had ignited you could have been killed.' Her voice hiccupped and she dissolved into tears again.

He caught her wrists with his damaged hands. 'Because I thought you were in there.'

She stilled. 'Me?'

'You weren't answering your phone. I was worried.'

The implication of his words slammed into her like the kind of fast, hard wave that knocked you down, leaving you to tumble over and over in the surf. His wife and son had been trapped inside a fire-ravaged building. What cruel fate had forced him to face such a scenario again? Suffer the fear that someone he cared for was inside?

She sniffed back her tears so she was able to speak. 'I'd gone to visit Ida. To talk...to talk business with her.' *And to mull over what a future without kids might mean.* 'I'm so sorry. It was my fault you—'

'It was my choice to go in there. I had to.'

His grip on her hands was so tight it hurt.

'All I could think about was how it would be if I lost you.'

He let go her hands and stepped back.

Something was wrong with this scenario. His

eyes, bluer than ever in the dark, smoke-dirtied frame of his face, were tense and unreadable. He fisted his hands by his sides.

She felt her stomach sink low with trepidation. 'But you didn't lose me, Ben. I'm here. I'm fine.'

'But what if you hadn't been? What if—?'

She fought to control the tremor in her voice. 'I thought we'd decided not to play the "what-if?" game.'

Beads of sweat stood out on his forehead. 'It was a shock.'

She heard the distant wail of a fire engine and was aware of people gathering at a distance from the shop.

Ben waved and called over to them. 'Nothing to worry about. Just smoke—no fire.'

He wiped his hand over his face in a gesture of weariness and resignation that tore at her. A dark smear of soot swept right across his cheek.

'Sandy, I need to let the fire department know they're not needed. Then go get cleaned up.'

'I'll come with you,' she said immediately.

This could be their last evening together.

He hesitated for just a second too long. 'Why don't you go back to the hotel and I'll meet you there?' he said.

One step forward and two steps back? Try ten steps forward and a hundred steps back.

'Sure,' she said, forcing the fear out of her voice. He went to drop a kiss on her cheek but she averted it so the kiss landed on her mouth. She wound her arms around his neck, clung to him, willing him with her kiss to know how much she cared for him. How much she wanted it to work out.

'Woo-hoo! Why don't you guys get a room?'

The call—friendly, well-meant—came from one of the onlookers. She laughed, but Ben glared. She dropped her arms; he turned away.

So she *wasn't* imagining the change in him.

She forced her voice to sound Sunny-Sandy-positive. 'Okay. So I'll see you back at the hotel.'

She headed back towards Hotel Harbourside, disorientated by a haunting sense of dread.

Ben hated the confusion and hurt on Sandy's face. Hated that he was the cause of it. But he felt paralysed by the fear of losing her. He needed time to think without her distracting presence.

Thanks to this special woman he'd come a long way in the last few days. But what came next? Sandy deserved commitment. Certainty. But there were big issues to consider. Most of all the make-or-break question of children. He'd been used to managing only his own life. Now Sandy was here. And she'd want answers.

Answers he wasn't sure he could give right now.

CHAPTER SIXTEEN

SANDY WAS JUST about to turn in to the hotel entrance when she stopped. It wasn't exactly anger towards Ben that made her pause. More annoyance that she was letting herself tiptoe around vital issues she and Ben needed to sort out if they were to have any hope of a future together.

Ben needed to be treated with care and consideration for what he'd been through. But she had to consider her own needs, too. Decision time was looming. If she was to go to Melbourne and interview for the candle shop franchise she had to leave here by the latest tomorrow morning.

She turned right back around and headed down the steps to the beach.

The heat was still oppressive, the sand still warm. At this time of year it wouldn't get dark until nearly nine.

Before the sun set she needed answers.

She found Ben sitting on the wooden dock that led out from the boathouse into the waters of the bay.

His broad shoulders were hunched as he looked out towards the breakwater.

Without a word she sat down beside him. Took his hand in hers. In response, he squeezed it tight. They sat in silence. Her. Ben. And that darn woolly mammoth neither of them seemed capable of addressing.

Beyond the breakwater a large cargo ship traversed the horizon. Inside the harbour walls people were rowing dinghies to shore from where their boats were anchored. A large seagull landed on the end pier and water slapped against the supporting posts of the dock.

She took a deep breath. 'Ida wants to sell me Bay Books.'

'Is that what you want?' His gaze was intent, the set of his mouth serious.

She met his gaze with equal intensity. 'I want to run my own business. I think I could make the bookshop work even better than it already does. But you're the only reason for me to stay in Dolphin Bay.'

'An important decision like that should be made on its own merits.'

'The bookshop proposition's main merit is that it allows me to stay here with you.' *Time to vanquish that mammoth.* 'We have to talk about where we go from here.'

His voice matched the bleakness of his face. 'I don't know that I can give you what you want.'

'I want you, Ben. Surely you know that.'

'I want you too. More than you can imagine. If it wasn't for…for other considerations I'd ask you to stay. Tell you to phone that candle guy and cancel your interview in Melbourne. But…but it's not that straightforward.'

'What other considerations?' she asked, though she was pretty sure she knew the answer.

He cleared his throat. 'I saw how you were with Amy.'

'You mean how I dote on her?'

He nodded. 'You were meant to be a mother, Sandy. Even when you were eighteen you wanted to have kids.'

'Two girls and a boy,' she whispered, the phrase now a desolate echo.

'I can't endure loss like that again. Today brought it all back.'

She wanted to shake him. Ben was smart, educated, an astute businessman. Why did he continue to run away from life? From love.

'I appreciate your loss. The pain you've gone through. But haven't you punished yourself enough for what happened?'

He made an inarticulate response and she knew she had hurt him. But this had been bottled up for too long.'

'Can't you see that any pleasure involves possible pain? Any gain possible risk. Are you *never* going to risk having your heart broken again?'

His face was ashen under his tan. 'It's too soon.'

'Do you think you'll ever change your mind about children?'

She held her breath in anticipation of his answer.

'Since you've been back I've thought about it. But four days isn't long enough for me to backtrack on something so important.'

Deep down she knew he was only giving voice to what she already knew. She wanted Ben. She wanted children. But she couldn't have both.

Slowly she exhaled her breath in a huge sigh. 'I can take that as a no then. But, Ben, you're only thirty-one. Too young to be shutting down your life.'

His jaw set in a stubborn line. 'It wouldn't be fair for me to promise something I can't deliver.'

'I…I understand.' But she didn't. Not really.

She shifted. The hard boards of the dock were getting uncomfortable.

'And I appreciate your honesty.'

His gaze was shrewd. 'But it's not good enough for you?'

She shook her head. 'No. It's not.'

Now she felt the floodgates were open. 'It was compromise all the way with Jason. I wanted marriage and kids. He said he had to get used to the idea. I moved in with him when I didn't want to live together without being married. Fine for other people. Too insecure for me. But I went along with him, put my own needs on hold.' Her attempt at laughter came out sharp-edged and brittle. 'Now I hear he's not only married, but his wife is pregnant.'

'That…that must have been a shock.'

'I can't go there again, Ben. Can't stay here waiting for heaven knows how long for you to get the courage to put the past behind you and commit to a future with me.'

Ben looked down at where the water slapped against the posts. She followed his gaze to see a translucent jellyfish floating by to disappear under the dock, its ethereal form as insubstantial as her dreams of a life with Ben.

'I'm sorry,' he said.

She didn't know whether he was apologising for Jason or because he couldn't give her the reassurances she wanted.

'I…I won't make all the compromises again, Ben,' she said brokenly. 'No matter how much I love you.'

She slapped her hand to her mouth.

The 'L' word.

She hadn't meant to say it. It had just slipped out.

Say it, Ben. Tell me you love me. Let me at least take that away with me.

But he didn't.

Maybe he couldn't.

And that told her everything.

'I'm sorry,' he said again, his voice as husky as she'd ever heard it. 'I can't be what you want me to be.'

If he told her she could do better than him she'd scream so loud they'd hear it all the way to New Zealand.

Instead he pulled her to him, held her tight against his powerful chest. It was the place she most wanted to be in the world. But she'd learned that compromise which was all one way wouldn't make either of them happy.

'I'm sorry too,' she murmured, fighting tears. 'But I'm not sorry I took that turn-off to Dolphin Bay. Not sorry we had our four-day fling.'

He pulled her to her feet. 'It's not over. We still have this evening. Tonight.'

She shook her head. 'It's perfect the way it is. I don't want to ruin the memories. I…I couldn't deal with counting down the hours to the last time we'll see each other.'

With fingers that trembled she traced down his cheek to the line of his jaw, trying to memorise every detail of his face. She realised she didn't have any photos to remember him by. Recalled there'd been a photographer at the dinner dance. She would check the website and download one. But not until she could look at his image and smile rather than weep.

'Sandy—' he started.

But she silenced him with a kiss—short, sweet, final.

'If you say you're sorry one more time I'll burst into tears and make a spectacle of myself. I'm going back to my room now. I've got phone calls to make. E-mails to send. Packing to do.'

A nerve flickered near the corner of his mouth. 'I'll call by later to…to say goodbye.'

'Sure,' she said, fighting to keep her voice under control. 'But I'm saying my goodbye now. No regrets. No what-ifs. Just gratitude for what we had together.'

She kissed him again. And wondered why he didn't hear the sound of her heart breaking.

Ben couldn't bear to watch Sandy walk away. He turned and made his way to the boathouse. Every step was an effort, as if he were fighting his way through a rip.

His house seemed empty and desolate—the home of a solitary widower. There was a glass next to the sink with Sandy's lipstick on the rim, but no other trace of her. He stripped off his smoke-stained clothes, pulled on his board shorts and headed for Big Ray Beach.

He battled the surf as if it were a foe, not the friend it had always been to him. He let the waves pound him, pummel him, punish him for not being able to break away from his self-imposed exile. The waves reared up over him, as if harnessing his anger at the cruel twist of fate that had brought Sandy back into his life but hadn't given him the strength to take the second chance she had offered him.

Finally, exhausted, he made his way back to the boathouse.

For one wild moment he let himself imagine what

it would be like to come back to the house to find Sandy there. Her bright smile, her welcoming arms, her loving presence.

But the house was bare and sterile, his footsteps loud and lonely on the floorboards. That empty glass on the draining board seemed to mock him. He picked up the photo of him and Sandy on the beach that long-ago summer. All their dreams and hopes had stretched out ahead of them—untainted by betrayal and pain and loss.

He put down the photo with its faded image of first love. He'd lost her then. And he'd been so damned frightened of losing her at some undefined time in the future he'd lost her now.

He slammed his fist down so hard on the dresser that the framed photo flew off the top. He rescued it from shattering on the floor only just in time.

What a damn fool he was.

He'd allowed the fears of the past to choke all hope for the future.

Sandy had offered him a second chance. And he'd blown it.

Sandy. Warm, vibrant, generous Sandy. With her don't-let-anything-get-you-down attitude.

That special magic she'd brought into his life had nothing to do with the glitter she trailed around with her. Sandy's magic was hope, it was joy, but most of all it was love.

Love he'd thought he didn't deserve. With bitterness and self-loathing he'd punished himself too harshly. And by not forgiving himself he'd punished Sandy, too.

The final rusted-over part of him shifted like the seismic movement of tectonic plates deep below the floor of the ocean. It hurt. But not as much as it would hurt to lose Sandy for good.

He had to claim that love—tell her how much she meant to him. Show her he'd found the courage and the purpose to move forward instead of tripping himself up by looking back.

He showered and changed and headed for the hotel.

Practising in his head what he'd say to her, he rode the elevator to Sandy's room. Knocked on the door. Once. Twice. But no reply.

'Sandy?' he called.

He fished out the master key from his wallet and opened the door.

She was gone.

The suitcase with all her stuff spilling out of it was missing. Her bedlinen had been pulled down to the end of the bed. There was just a trace of her vanilla scent lingering in the air. And on the desk a trail of that darn glitter, glinting in the coppery light of the setting sun.

In the midst of the glitter was a page torn out from the fairy notebook she always carried in her bag. It was folded in two and had his name scrawled on the outside.

His gut tightened to an agonising knot. With unsteady hands he unfolded the note.

Ben—thank you for the best four days of my life. I'm so glad I took a chance with you. No regrets. No 'what ifs'. Sandy xx.'

He fumbled for his mobile. To beg her to come back. But her number went straight to voicemail. Of course it did. She wouldn't want to talk to him.

He stood rooted to the ground as the implications of it all hit him.

He'd lost her.

Then he gave himself a mental shaking.

He could find her again.

It would take at least ten hours for her to drive to Melbourne. More if she took the coastal road. It wasn't worth pursuing her by car.

In the morning he'd drive to Sydney, then catch a plane to Melbourne.

He'd seek her out.

And hope like hell that she'd listen to what he had to say.

Sandy had abandoned her plan to mosey down the coastal road to Melbourne. Instead she cut across the Clyde Mountain and drove to Canberra, where she could connect to the more straightforward route of the Hume Highway.

She didn't trust herself to drive safely in the dark

after the emotional ups and downs of the day. A motel stop in Canberra, then a full day's driving on Thursday would get her to Melbourne in time to check in to her favourite hotel and be ready to wow the candle people on Friday morning.

She would need to seriously psyche herself up to sound enthusiastic about a retail mall candle shop when she'd fallen in love with a quaint bookshop on a beautiful harbour.

Her hands gripped tight on the steering wheel.

Who was she kidding?

It was her misery at leaving Ben that she'd have to overcome if she was going to impress the franchise owners.

She'd cried all the way from Dolphin Bay. Likely she'd cry all the way from Canberra to Melbourne. Surely she would have run out of tears by the time she faced the interview panel?

She pulled into the motel.

Ben would have read her note by now. Maybe it had been cowardly to leave it. But she could not have endured facing him again, knowing she couldn't have him.

No regrets. No regrets. No regrets.

Ben was her once-in-a-lifetime love. But love couldn't thrive in a state of inertia.

She'd got over Ben before. She'd get over him again.

Soon her sojourn in Dolphin Bay would fade into

the realm of happy memories. She had to keep on telling herself that.

And pray she'd begin to believe it.

CHAPTER SEVENTEEN

BEN REMEMBERED SANDY telling him about her favourite hotel in the inner-city Southbank district of Melbourne—all marble, chandeliers and antiques. He'd teased her that it sounded too girly for words. She'd countered that she liked it so much better than his preferred stark shades of grey.

He'd taken a punt that that was where she would be staying. A call to Reception had confirmed it. He walked from his ultra-contemporary hotel at the other end of the promenade that ran along the banks of the Yarra River. He'd wait all day at her hotel to see her if he had to.

It was a grey, rainy morning in Melbourne, mitigated by the brilliant colours of a myriad umbrellas. Ben watched a hapless duck struggling to swim across the wide, fast-flowing brown waters of the Yarra.

Was his mission doomed to such a struggle?

He found the hotel and settled in one of the comfortable velvet chairs in the reception area. He didn't have to wait for long. He sensed Sandy was there before he glanced up.

He was shocked at how different she looked. She wore a sleek black suit with a tight skirt that finished above her knees and high-heeled black shoes. A laptop in a designer bag was slung across her shoulder. Her hair was sleek, her mouth glossy with red lipstick.

She looked sexy as hell and every inch the successful businesswoman.

Sandy the city girl.

It jolted him to realise how much he'd be asking her to give up. Now she was back in her own world would she want to settle for running a small-town bookshop in Dolphin Bay?

She must have felt his gaze on her, and stopped mid-stride as he rose from the chair. He was gratified that her first reaction was a joyous smile. But then she schooled her face into something more neutral.

For a moment that seemed to stretch out for ever they stood facing each other in the elegant surrounds of the hotel. He had to get it right this time. There wouldn't be another chance.

Sandy's breath caught.

Ben.

Unbelievably handsome and boldly confident in a superbly cut charcoal-grey suit. Her surf god in the city. She had trouble finding her voice.

'What are you doing here?' she finally managed to choke out.

He stepped closer. 'I've come to tell you how much I love you. How I always loved the memory of you.'

Ben. This troubled, scarred man she adored. He had come all the way to Melbourne to tell her he loved her, smack in the middle of a hotel lobby.

She kept her voice low. 'I love you too. But it doesn't change the reasons why I left Dolphin Bay.'

'You gave me the kick in the butt I needed. I'm done with living with past scars. I want a future. With you.'

He looked around. Became aware they were attracting discreet interest.

'Can we talk?'

'My room,' she said.

They had the elevator to themselves and she ached to kiss him, to hold him. That would only complicate things, but for the first time she allowed herself a glimmer of hope for a future with Ben.

Ben was grateful for the privacy of Sandy's hotel room. He took both her hands in his. Pulled her close. Looked deep into her eyes. 'More than anything I want a life with you.'

'Me too, Ben.'

'That life would be empty without a child. *Our* child.'

He watched her face as the emotions flashed over it. She looked more troubled than triumphant.

'Oh, Ben, you don't have to say that. I don't want you to force yourself to do something so important as having children because you think it's what *I* want. That…that won't work.'

The fear he'd been living with for five years had been conquered by her brave action in walking away from him.

'It's for your sake, yes. But it's also for my own.' He took a deep breath. 'I want to be a dad again some day.'

The loss of Liam had been tragic. All potential for that little life gone in a terrible, pointless fire. But no matter how much he blamed himself, he knew deep in his gut he had not been responsible for those out-of-control flames. No one could have predicted how the wind had changed. No one could have saved Jodi and his son.

'I know you were a brilliant father in the little time you were granted with Liam. Everyone told me that.'

'I did my best.'

The four words echoed with sudden truth.

He deserved a second chance. Another son. A daughter. A baby who would grow into a child, like Amy, and then a teenager like he and Sandy had been when they met. It would not diminish the love he'd felt for Jodi and Liam.

'I want a family again, Sandy, and I want it with you. We'll be good parents.'

Exulting, he kissed her—a long, deep kiss. But there was more he needed to talk about before he could take her back home with him. He broke the kiss, but couldn't bear to release her hands from his.

'How did your interview go?' he asked.

'The Melbourne store is mine if I want it.' She was notably lacking in enthusiasm.

'*Do* you want it? Because if your answer is yes I'll move to Melbourne.'

Her eyes widened. 'You'd do that?'

'If it's what it takes to keep you,' he said.

She shook her head. 'Of course I don't want it. I want to buy Bay Books from Ida and knock through into the space next door to make a bookshop/café. I want to have author talks. Cooking demonstrations. A children's storyteller.'

The words bubbled out of her—and they were everything he wanted to hear.

'I want to ask Ida to order matching carvings for the café from her Balinese woodcarver.'

'That can be arranged. I own the café. The lease is yours.' He ran his finger down her cheek to the corner of her mouth. 'Will you come back to Dolphin Bay with me?'

Sandy was reeling from Ben's revelations. But he hadn't mentioned marriage—and she wanted to be married before she had children.

She'd feared he was too damaged to love again—and look what had happened. What was to stop her proposing?

'Yes,' she said. 'I want to come back to Dolphin Bay. Be with you. But I—'

He silenced her with a finger over her mouth. 'One more thing.'

'Yes?' she said.

'Life is short. There's no time to waste. We could date some more. Live together. But I'd rather we made it permanent. Marry me?'

In spite of all his pain and angst and loss he'd come through it strong enough to love again. To commit.

But she didn't kid herself that Ben's demons were completely vanquished. He'd still need a whole lot of love, support and understanding. As his wife, she could give it to him by the bucketload. Ben still had scars—and she'd help him to heal.

'Yes, I'll marry you. Yes, yes and *yes*.'

He picked her up and whirled her around until she was dizzy.

They were laughing and trying to talk at the same time, interspersing words with quick, urgent kisses.

'I don't want a big white wedding,' she said.

'I thought on the beach?'

'Oh, yes! In bare feet. With Amy as a flower girl. And Hobo with a big bow around his neck.'

Her fairy notebook would be filling up rapidly with lists.

'We can live in the boathouse.'

'I'd love that.'

'Build a big, new house for when we have kids.'

Maybe it was because her emotions had been pulled every which way, but tears welled in her eyes again. Ben had come so far. And they had so far to go together.

She blinked them away, but her voice was wobbly when she got the words out. 'That sounds like everything I've ever dreamed of...'

She thought back to her goals, written in pink. *Tick. Tick. Tick.*

* * * * *

LARGER-PRINT BOOKS!

GET 2 FREE LARGER-PRINT NOVELS PLUS

2 FREE GIFTS!

✦ HARLEQUIN®

Romance

From the Heart, For the Heart

YES! Please send me 2 FREE LARGER-PRINT Harlequin® Romance novels and my 2 FREE gifts (gifts are worth about $10). After receiving them, if I don't wish to receive any more books, I can return the shipping statement marked "cancel." If I don't cancel, I will receive 4 brand-new novels every month and be billed just $4.84 per book in the U.S. or $5.24 per book in Canada. That's a savings of at least 19% off the cover price! It's quite a bargain! Shipping and handling is just 50¢ per book in the U.S. and 75¢ per book in Canada.* I understand that accepting the 2 free books and gifts places me under no obligation to buy anything. I can always return a shipment and cancel at any time. Even if I never buy another book, the two free books and gifts are mine to keep forever.

119/319 HDN F43Y

Name (PLEASE PRINT)

Address Apt. #

City State/Prov. Zip/Postal Code

Signature (if under 18, a parent or guardian must sign)

Mail to the **Harlequin® Reader Service:**
IN U.S.A.: P.O. Box 1867, Buffalo, NY 14240-1867
IN CANADA: P.O. Box 609, Fort Erie, Ontario L2A 5X3

Want to try two free books from another line?
Call 1-800-873-8635 or visit www.ReaderService.com.

* Terms and prices subject to change without notice. Prices do not include applicable taxes. Sales tax applicable in N.Y. Canadian residents will be charged applicable taxes. Offer not valid in Quebec. This offer is limited to one order per household. Not valid for current subscribers to Harlequin Romance Larger-Print books. All orders subject to credit approval. Credit or debit balances in a customer's account(s) may be offset by any other outstanding balance owed by or to the customer. Please allow 4 to 6 weeks for delivery. Offer available while quantities last.

Your Privacy—The Harlequin® Reader Service is committed to protecting your privacy. Our Privacy Policy is available online at www.ReaderService.com or upon request from the Harlequin Reader Service.

We make a portion of our mailing list available to reputable third parties that offer products we believe may interest you. If you prefer that we not exchange your name with third parties, or if you wish to clarify or modify your communication preferences, please visit us at www.ReaderService.com/consumerschoice or write to us at Harlequin Reader Service Preference Service, P.O. Box 9062, Buffalo, NY 14269. Include your complete name and address.

HRLP13R

Enjoy this sneak preview of
THE RETURNING HERO,
the first in Soraya Lane's
THE SOLDIERS' HOMECOMING *duet!*

"LET ME STAY for a few days, let you catch up on some sleep while I'm here."

His voice was lower than usual, an octave deeper. She shook her head. "You don't have to do that. I'll be fine."

She might have been telling him no, but inside she was screaming out for him to stay. Having Brett here would make her feel safe, let her relax and just sleep solidly for a few nights at least, but she didn't expect him to do that.

And her intentions weren't pure, either. Because ever since she'd starting thinking about Brett in a certain way last night, remembering how soft his lips had been, how sensual it had been pressed against his body, she'd thought of nothing other than having him here. Keeping him close. Wondering if something could happen between them, and whether he wanted it as much as she did, even if she did know it was wrong.

"If I'm honest, Brett, having you here for a few days sounds idyllic." She wanted to stay strong, but she also wanted a man in her house again. Wanted the company of someone she could actually talk to, who wasn't afraid of the truth. Of what had happened to her husband. Because she had no one else to talk to, and no one else to turn to. She'd

HREXP0214

lost her dad and then her husband to war, and she was tired of being alone. "But only if you're sure."

She listened to Brett's big intake of breath, watched the way his body stiffened, then softened back to normal again.

"Then I'll stay. As long as you need me here, I'll stay."

She dropped her head to his shoulder. "He would have liked you being here. You know that, right?"

Brett shrugged, but she could tell he was finding this as awkward as she was. "You know, he made me promise to look out for you if anything ever happened to him. I just never figured that we'd actually be in that position."

Jamie smiled. "I'll never forget what you've done for me, Brett."

Brett was her friend. Nothing more. She just had to keep reminding herself of that, because falling in love with her husband's best buddy? Not something that could happen. Not now, not ever.

Brett could have been the man of her dreams—*once*. But now wasn't the time to look back. Now was about the future. The one she had to build without her husband by her side. No matter how much she was thinking about *that* kiss.

Don't miss THE RETURNING HERO by Soraya Lane, available March 2014. And look out for the second in this heartwarming duet, HER SOLDIER PROTECTOR, available April 2014.